生活情境會話 × 實用會話句型詳解

高頻率會話「例句」，

讀完 60 堂英文會話課，

讓你在短時間內就可以對任何人用英文侃侃而談。

User's Guide
使用說明

使用說明
POINT 1.

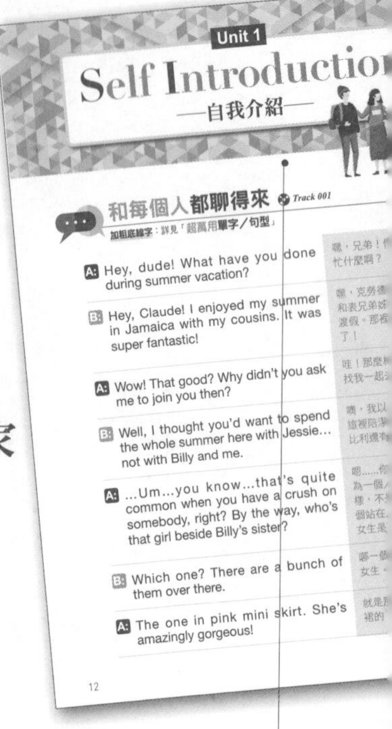
Unit 1
Self Introductio
—自我介紹—

和每個人都聊得來 Track 001
加粗底線字：詳見「超萬用單字／句型」

A: Hey, dude! What have you done during summer vacation?

B: Hey, Claude! I enjoyed my summer in Jamaica with my cousins. It was super fantastic!

A: Wow! That good? Why didn't you ask me to join you then?

B: Well, I thought you'd want to spend the whole summer here with Jessie… not with Billy and me.

A: …Um…you know…that's quite common when you have a crush on somebody, right? By the way, who's that girl beside Billy's sister?

B: Which one? There are a bunch of them over there.

A: The one in pink mini skirt. She's amazingly gorgeous!

12

幽默生動的實境會話，讓你有如身處英語系國家

本書共有 60 個 Unit，每一個 Unit 都以一則生動的實境會話開始，涵蓋生活、工作、學習、理財、旅遊、社交等各個生活情境，幫助你打造出最道地的英文口語環境，讓你不出國也能學會道地英文會話。

使用說明
POINT 2.  Track 001

外師親錄MP3，學會道地外國口音

全書皆由專業外籍老師親自錄音，可以反覆聆聽，練出道地發音和腔調。英文聽力、口說同時練習，兩種學習輕鬆滿足！

使用說明
POINT3.

超萬用句型詳解，更詳細解讀會話中的實用句型

文中以**粗字加底線**部分呈現的是使用率超高的實用句型，可以先聽聽這些句型在會話中的什麼時機使用，再參照會話下方的超萬用句型詳解與例句，更詳細地學習常用會話句型。

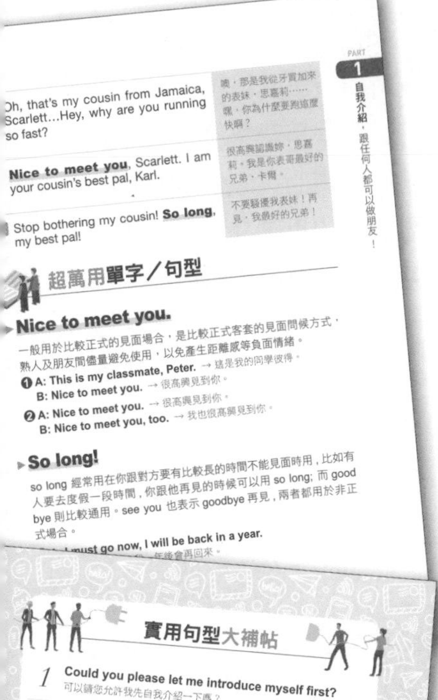

PART 1 自我介紹，跟任何人都可以做朋友！

Oh, that's my cousin from Jamaica, Scarlett…Hey, why are you running so fast?	噢，那是我從牙買加來的表妹，思嘉莉……嘿，你為什麼要跑這麼快啊？
Nice to meet you, Scarlett. I am your cousin's best pal, Karl.	很高興認識妳，思嘉莉。我是你表哥最好的兄弟，卡爾。
Stop bothering my cousin! **So long**, my best pal!	不要騷擾我表妹！再見，我最好的兄弟！

超萬用單字／句型

Nice to meet you.

一般用於比較正式的見面場合，是比較正式客套的見面問候方式，熟人及朋友間儘量避免使用，以免產生距離感等負面情緒。

1. A: This is my classmate, Peter. → 這是我的同學彼得。
   B: Nice to meet you. → 很高興見到你。
2. A: Nice to meet you. → 很高興見到你。
   B: Nice to meet you, too. → 我也很高興見到你。

So long!

so long 經常用在你跟對方要有比較長的時間不能見面時用，比如有人要去度假一段時間，你跟他再見的時候可以用 so long; 而 good bye 則比較通用。see you 也表示 goodbye 再見，兩者都用於非正式場合。

I must go now, I will be back in a year.

使用說明
POINT4.

實用句型大補帖，一個情境學到更多用法

從生活情境中的各種方面嚴選其他常見句型，絕對是老外對話時的道地用法。仔細多讀幾遍，各種情境的每種狀況都可以開口說出恰當的英文！

實用句型大補帖

1. **Could you please let me introduce myself first?**
   可以請您允許我先自我介紹一下嗎？
2. **Please allow me to introduce the new comer of our company.**
   請容我介紹我們公司的新員工。
3. **Which university did you graduate from and what's your major?**
   你畢業於哪所大學，主修是什麼？
4. **What do you do?**
   你是做什麼工作的？
5. **I can't believe we've meet each other again here!**
   沒想到我們竟然在這裡又碰面了！
6. **How are you? It's been a long time since we last meet.**
   你好嗎？距離我們上一次見面已經有段時間了。
7. **Mom, this is my classmate, Lucy Green, you can call her Lucy.**
   媽，這是我的朋友露西．格林，可以叫她露西。
8. **I'm glad to meet you, please send our regards to your parents.**
   很高興見到你，請代我們向你的父母問好。
9. **Oh, you are David's teacher? So are you familiar with his parents?**
   噢，你是大衛的老師嗎？那你跟他家長熟嗎？

Preface
前言

大家好，很高興你翻到這本實用的英語會話書！我常遇到許多學習英文的讀者和我說：明明已經學那麼多年的英文，為什麼開口說英文那麼困難？相信正在閱讀此頁的你，內心一定有一個夢想——**希望有一天能輕鬆自在的用英文和老外聊天，想說什麼就說什麼，甚至是任何場合都能開口大聲說。**我寫這本書的目的，就是希望讓有「英文會話恐懼症」的人，在國外旅遊時可以自己買票、點餐，在工作時可以自信的和客戶侃侃而談，在認識外國朋友時可以天南地北無所不聊，甚至是迷路、試穿衣服、看醫生等各種臨時情況都能自己用英文解決。

試著想想看，當你和老外交談時、旅遊時、遇到緊急狀況時，真的有時間拿出手機查英文單字或會話句子嗎？想要隨時開口說英文，就給自己一次機會，透過本書的60堂英文會話課，一網打盡生活、工作、學習、理財、旅遊、社交等60個幽默寫實的英文會話情境吧！

本書除了愈讀愈有趣、令人欲罷不能的生活情境會話外，每篇的**英文會話「例句」補充篇，句句選用最實用的高頻率例句，讓你更貼近老外開口時的道地用法**，並可以迅速在最短的時間內，將老外都在說的英文會話短句深植腦海。每篇清楚明確的情境分類，幫助你立即掌握會話例句使用的時機和狀態，讓你在對的時機，開口說出適當的英文。

會話部份之外，我在本書的每一篇都特別設計了實用的**「超萬用句型」，讓你在會話外，更深入學習句型的靈活使用方式、增強會話的能力**；在兼顧文法正確性之下，讓同一句話百變自如。開口說得出有變化的句子，加上更靈活的用法，讓你說出的英文不再無聊；不再像教科書一樣呆板，也不會每次老外和你打招呼都只會回答：「I'm fine, thank you, And you?」

英文是「實用」的語言，除了學會文法、單字等知識外，還要學會如何「運用」。希望各位讀者透過本書，找到一條學好英文會話的捷徑，面對任何人都能輕鬆開口，以流利、道地的英文和老外對話！

Content
目錄

Part4 餐廳用餐，用餐大小事都能對任何人清楚說！

Part5 美髮美體，在國外美容隨時都能開口用英文聊！

Part6 談情說愛，國籍不是問題、外國男／女友手到擒來！

Part 7 聊天哈啦，絕不錯過和任何人用英文閒聊的好時機！

Part 8 投資理財，搞懂財經英文口語、在哪裡都能做好財務規劃！

Part 9 遭遇難題，出國在外，向任何人開口求救都不是問題！

Part 10 歡慶節日，搞懂節日文化、和任何人都可以相約歡慶節日！

Part 1

自我介紹，跟任何人都可以做朋友！

Unit 1

Self Introduction

──自我介紹──

和每個人都聊得來 Track 001

加粗底線字：詳見「超萬用單字／句型」

A: Hey, dude! What have you done during summer vacation?	嘿，兄弟！你暑假都在忙什麼啊？
B: Hey, Claude! I enjoyed my summer in Jamaica with my cousins. It was super fantastic!	嘿，克勞德！暑假時我和表兄弟姊妹在牙買加渡假。那裡真是太棒了！
A: Wow! That good? Why didn't you ask me to join you then?	哇！那麼棒？你怎麼沒找我一起去？
B: Well, I thought you'd want to spend the whole summer here with Jessie… not with Billy and me.	噢，我以為你會想留在這裡陪潔西，而不是跟比利還有我一起。
A: ...Um...you know...that's quite common when you have a crush on somebody, right? By the way, who's that girl beside Billy's sister?	嗯……你也知道嘛……為一個人著迷時就會這樣，不是嗎？對了！那個站在比利妹妹旁邊的女生是誰啊？
B: Which one? There are a bunch of them over there.	哪一個？那裡有那麼多女生。
A: The one in pink mini skirt. She's amazingly gorgeous!	就是那個穿粉紅色迷你裙的，她超迷人！

B: Oh, that's my cousin from Jamaica, Scarlett...Hey, why are you running so fast?	噢，那是我從牙買加來的表妹，思嘉莉……嘿，你為什麼要跑這麼快啊？
A: **Nice to meet you**, Scarlett. I am your cousin's best pal, Karl.	很高興認識妳，思嘉莉。我是你表哥最好的兄弟，卡爾。
B: Stop bothering my cousin! **So long**, my best pal!	不要騷擾我表妹！再見，我最好的兄弟！

超萬用單字／句型

▸ Nice to meet you.

一般用於比較正式的見面場合，是比較正式客套的見面問候方式，熟人及朋友間儘量避免使用，以免產生距離感等負面情緒。

❶ **A: This is my classmate, Peter.** → 這是我的同學彼得。
B: Nice to meet you. → 很高興見到你。

❷ **A: Nice to meet you.** → 很高興見到你。
B: Nice to meet you, too. → 我也很高興見到你。

▸ So long!

so long 經常用在你跟對方要有比較長的時間不能見面時用，比如有人要去度假一段時間，你跟他再見的時候可以用 so long; 而 good bye 則比較通用。see you 也表示 goodbye 再見，兩者都用於非正式場合。

❶ **A: I must go now, I will be back in a year.**
→ 我必須要走了，我一年後會再回來。
B: OK, so long. → 好的，再見。

❷ **A: Please call me when you are in Paris.**
→ 你到達巴黎後請打電話給我。
B: So long. → 再見。

實用句型大補帖

1 **Could you please let me introduce myself first?**
可以請您允許我先自我介紹一下嗎？

2 **Please allow me to introduce the new comer of our company.**
請容我介紹我們公司的新員工。

3 **Which university did you graduate from and what's your major?**
你畢業於哪所大學，主修是什麼？

4 **What do you do?**
你是做什麼工作的？

5 **I can't believe we've meet each other again here!**
沒想到我們竟然在這裡又碰面了！

6 **How are you? It's been a long time since we last meet.**
你好嗎？距離我們上一次見面已經有段時間了。

7 **Mom, this is my classmate, Lucy Green, you can call her Lucy.**
媽，這是我的朋友露西．格林，可以叫她露西。

8 **I'm glad to meet you, please send our regards to your parents.**
很高興見到你，請代我們向你的父母問好。

9 **Oh, you are David's teacher? So are you familiar with his parents?**
噢，你是大衛的老師嗎？那你跟他家長熟嗎？

Unit 2

At the Office

——職場——

和每個人都聊得來 Track 002

加粗底線字：詳見「超萬用單字／句型」

A: Good morning. I am the new English secretary, Caroline Wood.	早安，我是新報到的英文秘書，卡洛琳·伍德。
B: Good morning, this is the office of the Sales Department. I am Anthony Klein, Executive Assistant of the Manager. Let me introduce you to the office and our members.	早安，這裡是業務部辦公室。我是經理的行政助理，安東尼·克萊恩。讓我來為妳介紹我們辦公室和辦公室成員。
B: This is the office of the Manager, David Lawson. You'll talk to him later.	這是我們公司經理，大衛·勞森的辦公室。妳待會要和他談談。
A: Ok, I will get prepared before talking to him.	好的，在與經理談談前我會先準備一下。
B: First, let's get acquainted with the other members of the team. This way, please.	首先，讓我們先來認識一下團隊的其他成員。這邊請。
A: Thank you.	謝謝。
B: **Please allow me to** introduce the new English secretary, Caroline Wood.	請容我介紹一下新上任的英文秘書卡洛琳·伍德小姐。
A: I have just started working as an English secretary. Nice to meet you all.	這是我初次擔任英文秘書，請大家多指教！

B: Welcome to the Sales Department. We are pleased to have such a qualified member as you.	歡迎加入業務部，我們很高興有妳這樣能力出眾的成員加入！
A: Thanks. It's also my pleasure to join in the Sales Department.	謝謝。加入業務部也是我的榮幸。
B: I'm your superior. Please come to me if you have any questions, I will help you **get up to speed** quickly.	我是你的上司，如果有任何問題請來找我，我會幫助妳儘快進入狀態。

超萬用單字／句型

▶Get up to speed

get up to speed 是一種俚語的表達方式，用處非常廣泛，可用於工作及日常朋友相處中，意為「進入狀態；瞭解……」。

❶ **A: I hope you can get up to speed quickly.**
→我希望你能快速進入狀態。
B: OK, I will work hard on it. →好，我會努力的。

❷ **A: I will help you to get up to speed.** →我會幫助你瞭解狀況。
B: Oh, that's so kind of you. Thank you very much.
→ 哇，你人真好，非常感謝。

▶Please allow me to...

Please allow me to... 是一種非常客氣、委婉、有禮貌的表達請求及願望的方式，通常用於相對正式的場合。相同意義的還有「let me...」。

❶ **A: Mr. Green, please allow me to introduce my wife, Catherine.**
→ 格林先生，請允許我向您介紹我的夫人，凱薩琳。
B: Nice to meet you, Catherine. →很高興見到您，凱薩琳。

❷ **A: Now please allow me to congratulate you on your promotion.**
→ 現在請允許我對你的晉升表示熱烈的祝賀。
B: Thank you very much. → 非常感謝你。

實用句型大補帖

1 **You could find a wealth of information on our company website.**
您在我們的公司網站可以找到豐富的資訊。

2 **After the meeting, Lucy will give you the rundown on how the computer works.**
會議後，露西將為你做電腦功能的概述。

3 **I ought to introduce you to our manager after the meeting, so please wait a moment.**
我應於會議結束後把你介紹給經理，所以請稍等一下。

4 **How long have you been working here, Sam?**
山姆，你在這裡工作了多久？

5 **We will have a meeting later, and I will introduce you to all the employees. Please be prepared.**
我們待會要開會，屆時我會將你介紹給所有員工，請準備一下。

6 **OK, I hope we can get acquainted with each other sooner and work together in the future.See you.**
好，希望我們可以早點熟悉彼此，並且在將來合作愉快，再會。

Unit 3

Academy

——學業——

和每個人都聊得來 Track 003

加粗底線字：詳見「超萬用單字／句型」

A: Hi, is this seat available?	嗨！請問這個位子可以坐嗎？
B: Yeah, sure. I'm Mike from Utah, I major in mechanical engineering. What about you?	當然可以。我是來自猶他州的麥克。主修機械工程，妳呢？
A: **I'm from** California. I'm Jane, and I major in history.	我來自加州。我叫珍，主修歷史。
B: It's my first course about literature. Do you know anything about this course?	這是我第一堂文學課程。妳知道任何有關這門課的事嗎？
A: Well, it's necessary to attend every class, and always turn in the report before the deadline.	嗯，你必須要出席每堂課，而且準時交報告。
B: Is students' attendance counted in the final grades?	出席率會被列入期末成績考核嗎？
A: You can skip any class, but only if you can **keep up with** the studies.	你可以試試看翹課，但你得跟得上進度才行。

B: Is it easy to fail the exam and be flunked?	這門課很容易考試不及格然後被當掉嗎？
A: Um...depends on how often you'd come and how hard you'd study.	嗯……這就要看你有多常來上課，還有你唸書唸得多努力了。

超萬用單字／句型

▶ I'm from...

常用於陌生人介紹自己來自於哪裡，意為「來自於……」，在意義上等同於 I come from。

❶ **A: Where are you from?**
→你是哪裡人？
B: I'm from Japan.
→我來自日本。

❷ **A: The watch comes from Switzerland.**
→這手錶來自於瑞士。
B: Really? I don't think so.
→真的嗎？我不這麼認為。

▶ I can't keep up with ...

keep up with 意為「趕上」，通常用於學業中，表示能夠跟得上老師及教授的授課進度。

❶ **A: You're talking too fast. I can't keep up with you.**
→你講太快了，我跟不上。
B: Sorry. Would you like me to repeat that again?
→ 抱歉喔，那你要我再講一次嗎？

❷ **A: I can't keep up with the teacher. What should I do?**
→ 我跟不上老師的進度，我該怎麼辦呢？
B: You can borrow my notes.
→你可以借我的筆記。

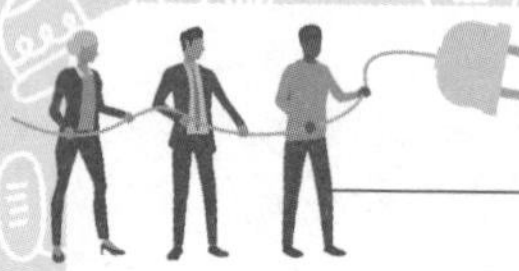

實用句型大補帖

1 **It's my first day at school, so could you please tell me where the student restaurant is?**
這是我第一天上學，你可以告訴我學生餐廳在哪裡嗎？

2 **Do you know anything about the compulsory courses?**
你知道必修課的事嗎？

3 **Oh my! I flunked the final exam!**
天哪！我期末考不及格！

4 **I've failed my exam.**
我考試沒過。

5 **I want to take a course in literature next semester.**
我下學期想修一門文學課。

6 **What if I don't turn in the report before the deadline?**
如果我沒有在期限內交報告會怎樣？

7 **Mike specializes in English in university, and after that he wants to study French.**
麥克在大學主修英文，之後他又想學習法文。

8 **Miss Brown, you're late to class again. Could you give me an account of what happened?**
布朗小姐，妳上課又遲到了，妳能解釋一下是怎麼回事嗎？

9 **What's your major? Do you like your professors?**
你主修什麼？你喜歡你的教授嗎？

10 **I sit in on Professor Wang's linguistic class every Thursday.**
我每個禮拜四都會旁聽王教授的語言學。

11 **Let's skip this class!**
我們翹掉這堂課吧！

12 **There is a midterm exam and a final exam in this course.**
這門課有期中考和期末考。

13 **Do you know why the math class was called off?**
你知道為什麼數學課會停課嗎？

14 **I'm the most likely person to be flunked!**
我是最有可能被當掉的人！

Part 2

出國旅行，

所有狀況跟任何人
都對答如流！

Unit 1

On the Way

——旅途景色——

和每個人都聊得來 Track 004

加粗底線字：詳見「超萬用單字／句型」

A: Excuse me, I lost my way. **How do I get to** the museum?	不好意思，我迷路了。請問博物館怎麼走？
B: Which museum do you want to go to?	妳要去哪一間博物館呢？
A: I would like to go to the Palace Museum.	我想去故宮博物院。
B: Well…I just moved to this city one month ago. I know it's not too far from here…	嗯……我一個月前才剛搬來這個城市。我知道故宮博物院離這不遠……
A: Do you suggest that I take a taxi?	你會建議我搭計程車嗎？
B: Yeah, it's safer and they don't charge high taxi fares in this city.	嗯，比較安全，而且這裡的計程車費不貴。
A: Taxi!	計程車！（舉手招計程車）
B: Hi, miss. Where would you like to go?	小姐，妳要去哪裡呢？
A: To the Palace Museum, please.	請到故宮博物院。

(A while later…)	（一陣子後……）
B: Here we are. Thirteen dollars, please.	我們到了。一共是13元。
A: Here's fifteen. Please **keep the change.**	這是15元，不用找了。

超萬用單字／句型

▶ How do I get to...?

此句型主要是陌生人在陌生城市，向對方打聽路線及旅遊景點的固定句型。意為「去……怎麼走？」，相同意義的表達方式還有「Where is the...? Could you tell me the way to...? Can you direct me to the...?」。

A: Do you know how I can get to the bus station?
→ 請問你知道怎麼去公車站嗎？

B: You can turn right and walk one block, and you will find the bus station. → 你可以右轉，走過一個街區，然後你就會看到公車站。

▶ keep the change.

字面直譯為「不用找零了。」，實則是歐美西方國家及日本等一些國家顧客付給飯店、餐廳、旅館以及計程車司機等服務人員的小費，數額根據國別的不同而有一定的差別。起源於 18 世紀英國倫敦，現已成為上述國家一種普通並禮貌的行為。

❶ **A: Thirty euros in total, sir.**
→ 先生，一共三十歐元。

B: Thanks. Keep the change, please.
→ 非常感謝，不用找零了。

❷ **A: Here's fifty dollars. Keep the change.**
→ 這是五十美元，不用找零了。

B: Thanks, sir. Good luck.
→ 先生，謝謝，祝你好運。

實用句型大補帖

1 **Excuse me? I lost my way. Could you tell me where the museum is?**
不好意思，我迷路了，請問博物館怎麼走？

2 **Could you please take me to the railway station?**
你能把我帶到火車站嗎？

3 **How do you charge the taxi fare here?**
這裡的計程車怎麼計費？

4 **How long will you be staying in the United States?**
你預計在美國停留多長時間？

5 **I want to book one economy class seat to Paris.**
我要訂一張去巴黎的經濟艙座位。

6 **Not only my bags but also a medium-sized suitcase was lost.**
不只我的包包，還有一個中型皮箱也不見了。

7 **Are you here on business or for sightseeing?**
你是來出差還是來觀光的？

8 **I am leaving for Barcelona tonight. Tomorrow I will be there on time .**
我今晚將動身到巴賽隆納，明天會準時到達。

9 **Do you have a return ticket?**
你有回程機票嗎?

Unit 2

Accomodation

——住宿——

和每個人都聊得來 Track 005

加粗底線字：詳見「超萬用單字／句型」

A: I've booked a standard room on the website. Could you check for me?	我在網站預訂了一間標準房，可以幫我查一下嗎？
B: My pleasure. **May I have your name**, Sir?	很榮幸為您服務。請問您的大名？
A: Elk Smith. By the way, the reservation was on June 22nd.	艾爾克．史密斯。對了！我是在6月22日預約的。
B: Ok, hold on a second, please. I'll check for you.	Ok，請稍等一下。讓我幫您查查。
(1 minute later)	（一分鐘後）
B: I couldn't find your name, sir. Could you please fill in the registration form?	我沒看到您的大名。可以請您填一下入住登記表嗎？
A: What? Then is there any similar room available?	什麼！那你們還有相似的空房間嗎？
B: Yes, the housekeeper is cleaning the room for you now. You may check in in 5 minutes.	有的。清理人員已經在幫您打掃房間了。您可以在5分鐘後入住。

A: Should I **settle my bill** right now?	我需要現在付款嗎？
B: Yes, please. Your room number is 303. Here's the key card. Good day.	是的。您的房間號碼是303，這是您的房間感應卡。預祝您有美好的一天！

超萬用單字／句型

▸ May I have your name?

此句多用於飯店和旅館等服務場所，服務人員向顧客詢問登記入住姓名的固定用法，意為「您的姓名是？」本句為服務行業的專業用法，一般場合的詢問姓名不用此句。

❶ **A : Welcome to Hilton Hotel. May I have your name?**
→ 歡迎光臨希爾頓酒店，方便告訴我您的姓名嗎？
B : I'm David; I have reserved a room two days ago.
→ 我是大衛，兩天前我預定了房間。

❷ **A : May I have your name, sir?** → 先生，請問您叫什麼？
B : My name is Paul, P-A-U-L. → 我叫保羅，P-A-U-L。

▸ Can I settle my bill?

此句通常用於飯店及旅館顧客需要退房時對服務人員所說的話，意為「可以結帳嗎？」，相同情景的表達方式還有「I'd like to settle my bill.」。

❶ **A: Can I settle my bill now?** → 我現在能結帳嗎？
B: Of course, may I have your name? → 當然，您的姓名是？

❷ **A: I'd like to settle my bill.** → 我想結帳退房。
B: Certainly, sir. May I have your room number, please?
→ 好的，先生，請把房間號碼給我好嗎？

實用句型大補帖

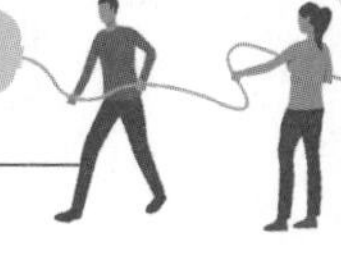

1 **Could you hold the line , please? I'll check our room availability.**
請您稍等，待我檢查一下這段時間是否有空房。

2 **Could you please fill in the registration form, sir?**
先生，可以請您填寫一下這張登記表嗎？

3 **I would like to book a room with two beds. Could you check for me?**
我想預訂有兩張床的房間，你能幫我查看一下嗎？

4 **Is there any room available? I'd like to check in.**
請問有空房間嗎？我想辦理住宿登記。

5 **Your reservation is for a standard room with a double bed, right?**
您要一間雙人床的標準房，對嗎？

6 **Your room number is 031. Here's the key. If you have any questions, please call me.**
您的房間號是031，這是您的鑰匙，如有任何問題請打電話給我。

7 **The housekeeper will clean your room at ten o'clock.**
客房服務人員將在十點整時清理您的房間。

8 **This is Mary in Room 711. I'd like to order some food.**
我是711房間的瑪麗，我想點餐。

9 **Please come downstairs and pick up your buffet voucher.**
請下樓領取您的自助餐兌換券。

10 **Could you please book a room with a view of the sea for me?**
能幫我訂有海景的房間嗎？

11 **Please wait a moment. I will call the manager.**
請稍等，我打電話給經理。

Unit 3

Tourist Spots

——景點——

和每個人都聊得來 *Track 006*

加粗底線字：詳見「超萬用單字／句型」

A: Good afternoon, do you have any information about sightseeing in the city?	午安，關於市區觀光請問您能提供什麼資訊嗎？
B: Good afternoon, do you have a travel brochure which you can take along ?	午安，請問您有隨身攜帶的觀光旅遊書手冊嗎？
A: What brochure? I have nothing that I can refer to... Should I find a local guide?	什麼手冊？我沒有任何可以參考的書……我應該要請一個當地導遊嗎？
B: Well...not exactly. The transportation in this city is quite convenient. Please take this.	嗯……應該不需要。市內交通很方便，請參考這本冊子。
A: Wow! A city travel brochure! A thousand thanks!	哇！一本旅遊手冊耶！太感謝了！
B: Our pleasure. You may follow the instructions and take a subway tour in the city.	很榮幸為您服務。您可以根據冊子上的指示搭地鐵來趟市內觀光。
A: **Yep!** By the way, may I **hitchhike to that town next to the city**?	好耶！對了，我可以搭便車到隔壁的小鎮嗎？
B: Um...usually we don't recommend tourists to do hitchhiking here.	嗯……通常我們不建議遊客搭便車旅遊。

A: Oh...I did it thousands of times in America though...	噢……可是我在美國都搭過超多次便車了耶……
B: But you are in Asia now, and hitchhiking isn't so popular here.	但現在您在亞洲，而且這裡不流行搭便車。

超萬用單字／句型

▶ hitchhike to + 地點

Hitchhiking 意為「搭便車」。指搭乘別人的車上路，分為免費和收費兩種。在歐美國家尤其是美國，搭便車是一種非常經濟、環保及實惠的旅行方式。

❶ **A: Once my friend and I tried hitchhiking, but no car stopped for us.** → 我和我的朋友曾經嘗試搭便車，但是沒有車停下來。

B: Oh, you are so unlucky. → 哇，你們好不幸啊！

❷ **A : I hope one day I can hitchhike to the coast.**
→ 我希望有一天我可以搭便車去海岸。

B: Really? I like that idea, too. → 真的嗎？我也喜歡這主意呢！

▶ Yep!

表示「是」等贊成對方的口吻，也可以表示欣賞他人説法做法的口吻，與 yes 的字面解釋相同，但是適用於網路、通常會話中使用。而且多用於同輩人，朋友之間。請不要用於長輩，因為 yep、yup 有點隨意、不太尊重的感覺。

❶ **A: Do you want to go to my hometown and visit my parents?**
→ 你願不願意到我的家鄉去拜訪我的父母？

B: Yep, when? → 好，什麼時候？

❷ **A: Lucy, come here. Let me tell you a secret.**
→ 露西，快過來，我告訴妳一個秘密。

B: Yep, what? → 好，什麼啊？

實用句型大補帖

1 **Could you take a photo for me here, please?**
能請你幫我在這裡照張相嗎？

2 **I need a local guide to introduce the tourist attractions.**
我需要一名當地導遊為我講解觀光景點。

3 **The Bund Tourist Tunnel connects the two best attractions of Shanghai: The Bund and Lu Jia Zui.**
外灘觀光隧道連接上海兩個最主要景觀：外灘和陸家嘴。

4 **I really want to take a tour of the White House, because it's the most famous historical building in the U.S.A.**
我真的很想去參觀一下白宮，因為它是美國最著名的歷史建築。

5 **If you don't have enough money to hire a tour guide, you can take along a travel brochure.**
如果你沒有足夠的錢請導遊，你可以隨身攜帶一本旅行小冊子。

6 **Summer is always a busy peak season for resorts in mountains and beaches.**
在山區和沿海地區的度假村，夏天總是人們的旅遊旺季。

7 **Do you have any information about the city sights?**
關於市區觀光，您有什麼資訊提供嗎？

8 **You'll see the world-famous magnificent waterfall soon.**
你馬上就會看到世界著名的瀑布奇觀了。

9 **Yep! Let's enjoy the wonderful view of the Seine.**
對，讓我們盡情欣賞塞納河的美景吧！

10 **Look at the lake. What a beautiful, peaceful lake!**
你看湖，這湖水太優美太平靜了。

Unit 4

Making Calls, Sending Mail & Currency Exchange

——通訊、郵件、外幣兌換——

和每個人都聊得來 Track 007

加粗底線字：詳見「超萬用單字／句型」

A: Hello, **Could I ask you a favor?**	哈囉，可以請你幫個忙嗎？
B: Yeah, what can I do for you?	好啊，您需要什麼？
A: Could you tell me where I should change my money?	可以告訴我在哪邊換錢嗎？
B: Oh, just go over there, see, on the left corner. There is a bank.	喔，就往那邊走，你看，左邊轉角那裡。那邊就有一家銀行。
A: Thanks so much. Have a good day!	太感謝了。祝你今天愉快！
(At the bank)	（在銀行）
B: May I help you?	您需要幫忙嗎？
A: Yeah. **Can I cash this check here?**	要，我可以在這邊兌換支票嗎？
B: Let me check for you, please. Please sign your name on the bottom line and put down your phone number.	我幫您確認一下。請在支票底端線上簽名並寫下您的電話號碼。

A: Thanks. And I also would like to know the exchange rate against dollars.	謝謝。然後我還想瞭解一下美金的匯率。
B: 1 euro can change into 1.09 dollars.	一歐元可以換1.09美元。
A: I would like to change $ 1,000 dollars into euro.	那我要把1000美元換成歐元。

超萬用單字／句型

▸Can I cash this check here?

此句多用於在外國出差旅行時，不想帶那麼多現金累贅，您可以選擇旅行支票或是雙幣信用卡。使用旅行支票就涉及到支票兌換的問題。此句多用於此，意為「這裡可以兌換支票嗎？」。

❶ **A: Can I cash this check here?** → 這裡可以兌換支票嗎？
B:Of course, we'd be happy to cash it for you.
→ 當然，我們很樂意為您兌現。

❷ **A: Can I cash this check here?** → 我能在這裡兌換支票嗎？
B: Sorry, sir, it's not business hour yet.
→ 不好意思，先生，現在還不是營業時間。

▸Could I ask you a favor?

此句多用於向別人請求幫助時，是一種非常客氣的標準美式表達法。意為「你能幫我個忙嗎？」，相同意義的表達方式還有「Would you please help me?」。

❶ **A: Could I ask you a favor?** → 能幫我個忙嗎？
B: What can I do for you? → 我能幫你什麼嗎？

❷ **A: Mom, could I ask you a favor?** → 媽，能幫我個忙嗎？
B: Of course I can. What happened?
→ 當然可以了，發生了什麼事？

實用句型大補帖

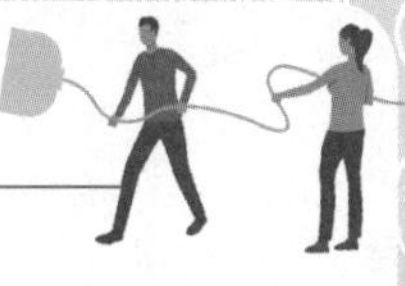

1 **Could you please change 10,000 euros into U.S. Dollars?**
可以請您幫我把一萬歐元兌換成美元嗎？

2 **I can't read English. Could I ask you a favor?**
我看不懂英文，可以請您幫個忙嗎？

3 **How would you like it, in US dollars or in euros?**
您要兌換成什麼，美元還是歐元？

4 **I'd like to mail this letter to Madrid via airmail.**
我要把這封信以航空的形式郵寄到馬德里。

5 **How long does it take for an airmail to get to Shanghai?**
寄往上海的航空信要多久才能到？

6 **How much does it cost to rent a post office box?**
租一個郵政信箱的費用是多少？

7 **Since he went to Paris, he has called his parents regularly.**
自從他到巴黎後，就定期打電話給他的父母。

8 **I must send a post card to Lily. I can't put it off any longer.**
我必須寄明信片給麗麗，不能再拖延了。

9 **My phone is running out of credits. Where can I go to buy more credits for my mobile?**
我的手機沒話費了，哪邊可以替我的手機購買加值呢？

10 **Please sign your name on the bottom line and put down your phone number.**
請在支票底端線上簽名並寫下您的電話號碼。

Part3
購物血拼，
在任何店家都可以
輕鬆開口！

Unit 1

Accessories
——首飾配件——

和每個人都聊得來 Track 008

加粗底線字：詳見「超萬用單字／句型」

A: Welcome to Hilton Jewelry. **What can I do for you**?	歡迎光臨希爾頓珠寶。有什麼可以為您效勞的嗎？
B: May my wife try on this pair of diamond earrings and that platinum necklace with rubies?	我老婆可以試戴這對鑽石耳環和那條鑲紅寶白金項鍊嗎？
A: Sure. This way, please. Here you are. They have a unique design and are popular now.	當然，請到這裡來。耳環和項鍊在這。它們設計獨特且是目前的流行款。
B: Oh… we think these seem rather old-fashioned after putting on. Could we see other collections?	噢……可是對我們來說戴起來感覺有點老氣。我們可以看看別組嗎？
A: How about those 18K gold necklaces with pearls? Feminine and gorgeous.	那些18K鑲珍珠的金項鍊如何？看起來很有女人味又高雅。
B: Um…Let us see.	嗯……讓我們看看。
A: What do you think about this collection?	您覺得這組戴起來如何呢？

B: Are these real pearls? I'm afraid that the luster will fade away…	這是鑲真的珍珠吧？我怕它會掉色。
A: We only offer customers the best quality jewelries and accessories.	我們只提供顧客最高品質的珠寶和配件。
B: Ok…then…**How much** are these? Do you offer discounts?	Ok……那麼，這些多少錢呢？有打折嗎？

超萬用單字／句型

▶ What can I do for you?

一般用於所有的以盈利為目的的營業機構，如商場、服飾店、首飾店及公司的總機等。意為「我能幫您什麼嗎？或者我能為您做些什麼？」，與此相同的表達方式還有「May I help you?」

❶ **A: Welcome to Hilton Hotel. What can I do for you?**
→ 歡迎光臨希爾頓酒店，我能幫您什麼嗎？
B: I want to book a presidential suit. → 我想訂一間總統套房。

❷ **A: What can I do for you, Sir?** → 先生，我能幫您什麼嗎？
B: Would you please change this to another one for me? It's too small. → 你能幫我再換一雙嗎？這雙太小了。

▶ How much...

一般用於購買場所，是表示詢問物品價格的表達方式，可用於對任何購買物品價格的詢問，意為「……多少錢？」或者「……的價錢是多少？」，是固定用法。

❶ **A: How much is it?** → 多少錢？
B: 50 euros in total. → 一共 50 歐元。

❷ **A: How much are the tomatoes per kilo?** → 番茄一公斤多少錢？
B: Two dollars. → 兩美元。

實用句型大補帖

1 **I prefer diamonds to pearls.**
我喜歡鑽石勝過珍珠。

2 **Tomorrow is Susan's birthday so I want to buy a gold ring for her. What do you think?**
明天是蘇珊的生日，我想為她買一個金戒指，你覺得怎麼樣？

3 **Do you know how to choose jewel earrings?**
你知道怎麼挑選寶石耳環嗎？

4 **What can I do for you, sir? We have 14K and 18K gold necklaces,chains and earrings.**
我能為您做些什麼，先生？我們店裡有14K和18K的金項鏈、手鏈和耳環。

5 **May I try this ruby ring on ?**
我可以試戴這件紅寶石戒指嗎？

6 **Would you please find me a pair of earrings that goes with my necklace?**
請問您能幫我找一對和我項鏈搭配的耳環嗎？

7 **How much does this platinum bracelet cost?**
這個白金手鐲多少錢？

8 **The design of this earring is very unique. However, I'm afraid that the luster will fade out .**
這個耳環的款式很別致，但是我擔心它的光澤會褪色。

9 **It seems too old-fashioned for me. Could I see another one, please?**
對於我來說，這個樣式太老氣了。我可以看看另一個嗎？

10 **It is the diamond ring that her husband gave to her.**
這就是她丈夫送給她的鑽戒。

Unit 2

Clothes

——服飾——

和每個人都聊得來 Track 009

加粗底線字：詳見「超萬用單字／句型」

A: Welcome to Emerald Boutique. May I help you?	歡迎來到翡翠精品。有什麼可以為您效勞的嗎？
B: I just want to look around first. Wait! May I take a look at that green dress?	我想先逛逛。等等！我可以看一下那件綠色洋裝嗎？
A: Sure, this dress is size M. **What size do you take**?	當然。這件是M號的。請問您穿什麼尺寸呢？
B: I am not quite sure. Could I have a try first?	我也不太確定耶。我可以先試穿吧？
A: Of course, the fitting room is around that corner. **This way, please**.	當然可以。試衣間在那邊的角落，請跟我來。
B: Oh…no… It's a little loose for me. May I try one in a smaller size?	噢……不……對我來說有點鬆。我可以試穿小一號的嗎？
A: I'm afraid it's impossible for we have only this one…How about this scarlet one of novel and fashionable design?	我想不行，我們只有這一件。要不然試試這件設計新穎、流行的這件緋紅洋裝好嗎？

B: Doesn't look too bad. Ok, I'll try this on.	看起來不錯。我試試。
A: It really fits you perfectly! Plus it's also on discount now.	真的很適合您！而且這件正在特價喔！
B: Oh! Excellent! This color makes me look brighter. I will get one.	噢！太棒了！這個顏色讓我看起來更明亮！我要這件。

超萬用單字／句型

▸What size do you take?

此句常用於在服飾店及鞋店等場合，服務人員詢問顧客尺寸等情境，意為「您穿什麼尺寸 (size) 的？」，相同意義的表達方式還包括「May I take your size? / What's your size?」

❶ **A: May I take your size, sir?** → 先生，您的尺寸是多少？
B: I don't know. Could you please let me have a try?
→ 我也不知道，你能先讓我試穿看看嗎？

❷ **A: What size do you take?** → 您穿幾號的？
B: Nine, maybe. → 或許是 9 號吧。

▸This way please!

一般出現於餐廳、飯店、服飾店及其他服務場所等，用於服務人員向顧客引路的固定用法，意為「請這邊走！」，相同意義的表達方式還有「Please follow me! 請跟我來！」。

❶ **A: Our manager is waiting for you. This way please!**
→ 我們經理正在等您，請這邊走！
B: OK, thank you very much! → 好，非常感謝！

❷ **A: Excuse me, could you please tell me where the restroom is?**
→ 打擾了，請問洗手間在哪裡？
B: Please follow me. → 請跟我來。

實用句型大補帖

1 **This shirt is size 8. I think it will fit you perfectly.**
這件襯衫的尺碼是8號，相信一定很適合您。

2 **I'm afraid we don't have it in your size.**
恐怕我們沒有您的尺寸。

3 **I would like to recommend this for you; it is novel and fashionable in design.**
我向您推薦這款，它的設計新穎時尚。

4 **I think it's out of date . Could I see a different one, please?**
我覺得這件過時了，我可以看另一件嗎？

5 **Here are three red ones in different shades. Which one do you like better?**
這是三種不同的紅色，你比較喜歡哪一種呢？

6 **The fitting room is just around the corner. This way please!**
試衣間在轉角處，請往這邊走！

7 **Could I have a lower price?**
能再算便宜一點嗎？

8 **I'm so sorry. There is no room for bargaining.**
非常抱歉，沒有議價的空間。

9 **If you really want to buy it, I can give you a 50 dollar discount.**
如果您真的想買的話，我可以算您便宜50美元。

10 **There are some jeans on sale .**
那裡有些牛仔褲在特賣。

11 **Hardly do I think it possible that this new pair of jeans has holes in the pockets. Please come back with your receipt tomorrow.**
我覺得這件新的牛仔褲幾乎不可能會有破洞，請明天帶著發票來。

12 **The button is missing. I'd like a refund.**
鈕扣掉了，我想退貨。

13 **There are so many different types. It's hard for me to pick out the one I like.**
有這麼多種不同的類型，對我來說實在太難選了。

Unit 3

Household Items

——居家用品——

和每個人都聊得來 Track 010

加粗底線字：詳見「超萬用單字／句型」

A: The washing machine is totally broken. It's time to get a fully automatic washing machine.	洗衣機完全壞了。我覺得是時候換一台全自動洗衣機了。
B: How about picking up one at the **flea market**?	要不要去跳蚤市場選一台呢？
A: Oh, no again! Remember that broken one? We got that at the flea market.	噢，不要再來了！記得那台壞掉的嗎？我們就是在跳蚤市場買的……
B: Ok. Let's get a brand new one at the mall then.	Ok。那我們去購物中心買台全新的吧！
(At the mall)	（在購物中心）
A: Hi, which brand of fully automatic washing machine is recommended? Could you tell us, please?	你好，請問有沒有什麼推薦的全自動洗衣機品牌呢？可以請你告訴我嗎？
B: I recommend you this new type of SnapX. It's almost sold-out!	我推薦SnapX 的全新款。幾乎要賣完了！
A: Let's read the instruction on this card…Oh! fantastic!	讓我們看看這張卡片的介紹吧……噢！太讚了！
B: Do you need further explanations about the SnapX 230 automatic washing machine?	請問還需要關於這台SnapX 230全自動洗衣機的進一步説明嗎？

A: Yeah…I'd like to know how long is the warranty for?	好啊……我想知道這台保固期多長？
B: You got the point! **It's good for** 3 years. Isn't it great?	您抓到重點了！它的保固期是3年，很棒吧？

超萬用單字／句型

▸ How long is it good for?

此句通常用於購買家電及其他機器設備時，用於向售貨員詢問商品的保固期限的固定用法。意為「……保固期有多久時間？」，相同意義的表達方式還有「How long is something's warranty for?」。

❶ **A: How long is this egg beater good for?**
→ 這台打蛋器的保固期多久？

B: It is good for ten years. → 這台打蛋器的保固期是 10 年。

❷ **A: I would like to ask how long it is good for?**
→ 我想問一下它的保固期是多久？

B: Wait for a moment. I'll show you the warranty card.
→ 請稍等，我給你看保固卡。

▸ flea market

關於 flea market，一種説法為最初來源於紐約的 Fly Market，Fly Market 是紐約下曼哈頓地區的一個固定市場。另一説法認為起源於 19 世紀末的法國，Le Marche aux Puces 是巴黎專門賣便宜貨的地方。這個詞是指在歐美及西方國家在週末郊外舉行的露天買賣市場，以經營舊貨及二手貨為主，意為「跳蚤市場」。

❶ **A: Have you ever been to a flea market during your stay in London?** → 你住在倫敦的時候去過跳蚤市場嗎？

B: Of course, I like to look around there.
→ 當然，我喜歡去那裡到處看看。

❷ **A: Oh, the old stamp looks so beautiful.**
→ 哇，這張舊郵票好漂亮啊。

B: You like it? I brought it in a flea market.
→ 你喜歡嗎？我是在跳蚤市場上買的。

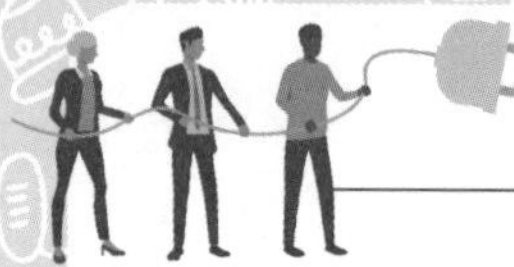

實用句型大補帖

1 **My children are fond of ice cream, so I want to know if the Hitachi refrigerators have a good freezer.**
我的孩子們喜歡吃冰淇淋，所以我想知道日立冰箱的冷凍系統好嗎？

2 **Would you like to go to the flea market with me?**
想和我一起去跳蚤市場嗎？

3 **What sort of material do you have for making pillowcases?**
你們有什麼適合做枕頭套的材料嗎？

4 **The oven is designed to burn out if it is overused, so please don't run a risk .**
此款烤箱被設計為過度使用就會燒毀，所以請千萬不要冒險。

5 **Our TV is broken. It's time for us to get a new one.**
我們的電視壞了，該是時候買台新的了。

6 **How long is this TV's warranty for?**
這台電視的保固期多久？

7 **Which brand of automatic rice cooker is the best? Could you recommend one to me?**
哪個牌子的電鍋是最好的？你能推薦一款給我嗎？

8 **We plan to buy some furniture this weekend. Would you like to join us?**
我們計畫在這週末去買一些傢俱用品，你想加入我們嗎？

9 **I would like to recommend this one to you. The resolution is great.**
我向您推薦這款電視機。它的畫質非常清晰。

10 **Do you have any blankets in your store?**
你們店裡有賣毛毯嗎？

11 **How long is it good for?**
它保固期多長？

Unit 4

Cosmetics & Daily Commodities
—化妝品 & 日用品—

和每個人都聊得來 Track 011

加粗底線字：詳見「超萬用單字／句型」

A: **To tell you the truth,** I kind of like your make-up and the smell of your perfume. Where did you get them?	説實話，我有點喜歡妳的妝和香水的味道耶，妳在哪裡買的呢？
B: They're from a big sale at the mall. I'm going there with Jamie later to get daily necessities. Wanna join us?	我在購物中心大拍賣買到的。待會我會和潔米去那裡採購生活用品，要一起去嗎？
A: Really? Count me in! I need to get some sunblock and lipsticks. I put on sunblock every time I go out.	真的嗎？算我一個！我必須去買防曬乳和唇膏了。我出門一定要擦防曬。
B: It's better to put on sunblock to protect your skin when doing outdoor activities.Good attitude!	恩，最好每次出門從事戶外運動都先塗抹防曬乳。妳很有概念！
A: **I can't agree with you more!**	我完全同意！
B: It's already 2 o'clock. Jamie's car is already down stairs.	已經快2點了，潔米的車已經在樓下了。
A: Really? Oh God! I haven't put on my make-up and sunblock...Can you wait for me for a minute?	真的嗎？天啊！我還沒化妝和擦防曬乳耶……妳們可以等我1分鐘嗎？

B: How many minutes do you need then? Your 1 minute is always 5 minutes...	妳到底需要幾分鐘啊？妳的1分鐘每次都是5分鐘……
A: Not this time...Please!	這次不會啦……拜託嘛！

超萬用單字／句型

▶ To tell (you) the truth, ...

外國人通常在想表達自己接下來所說的是句真話時會這麼使用，意思近似於中文的「老實說」、「說句真話」等。如：

❶ **A: I'm so sad now because Elle told me I'm ugly.**
→ 因為艾兒說我很醜，所以我很傷心。

B: To tell (you) the truth, you're the most beautiful girl I've ever met. → 說實話，你是我見過最美麗的女生了。

❷ **A: Why didn't you finish the exam paper?**
→ 你為什麼沒把考卷寫完？

B: To tell (you) the truth, I didn't study last night.
→ 老實說，我昨晚沒唸書。

▶ I can't agree with sb. more.

外國人在講話中常會這樣說來表示強烈的同意、同感，文意直翻為我不能同意你更多了，意思近似中文的「我完全同意」。

❶ **A: Mary is such a sweet girl who always helps others.**
→ 瑪莉真是個熱心助人的好女孩。

B: I can't agree with you more. → 我也這麼覺得。

❷ **A: We should replace our math teacher who punishes students a lot.** → 我們應該換掉老是處罰學生的數學老師。

B: I can't agree with you more. → 我完全同意。

實用句型大補帖

1 **I usually put on make-up every morning before I leave my dorm for work, but today I just ran out of cosmetics so I didn't put on any.**
我通常每天早上在從宿舍去上班前都會化妝，但今天因為化妝品用完了，所以我沒有化妝。

2 **No matter what his mother says, he still doesn't put on any sunblock.**
無論他媽媽說什麼，他仍然每天都不擦防曬乳。

3 **Hey, could you bring me some groceries?**
嘿，你能幫我帶些雜貨回來嗎？

4 **I know Daisy is a famous brand for high quality body lotions, but it's just too expensive for me to afford.**
我知道「雛菊」在高品質身體乳液中是知名品牌，但它實在貴到我負擔不起。

5 **When it comes to lipsticks, Cathy is an expert in choosing colors that match your outfit.**
說到口紅，凱西在挑選最搭配服裝的口紅顏色方面是個專家。

6 **Mom, we're running out of toilet paper in the restroom. Can you go to the supermarket and buy some?**
媽，我們的洗手間衛生紙用完了。妳可不可以再去超級市場買一些？

7 **Does your son also have a sweet tooth? Well, I guess we should both put the cookies back on the market shelves.**
你的兒子也愛吃甜食嗎？嗯，我想我們倆都應該把餅乾放回超市架上。

8 **Terry and I are going to the mall to buy some daily necessities. Do you want anything?**
泰瑞和我要去購物商場買些生活必需品，你有想要些什麼嗎？

9 **The news reported yesterday that hair gel isn't good for your health. I can't agree with it more. You should put it back.**
昨天的新聞報導說髮膠對健康不好，我完全同意。你最好把它放回去。

Unit 5

Digital Appliances

—3C產品—

和每個人都聊得來 Track 012

加粗底線字：詳見「超萬用單字／句型」

A: Welcome to 3C Paradise! What are you looking for? **If you need anything, just let me know.**	歡迎來到3C天堂，您想找什麼？如果有任何需要請跟我說！
B: Hi, I am looking for a computer. It doesn't need to be fancy, I only use it for the Internet and some documents.	我在找一台電腦。不用很新潮，我只用它上網和處理文件。
A: Well, which do you prefer, a desktop or a laptop?	嗯，您比較想要桌電還是筆電呢？
B: Which one do you think best meets my needs?	你覺得哪一種比較符合我的需求？
A: Um...A desktop usually has more functions, but if you need to run around often, I would suggest a laptop which suits you more.	嗯……桌電的功能比較多。但您如果經常外出，我會推薦您買筆電。
B: Oh...let me think for a second...	噢……讓我想一下……
A: Or maybe you would like to try a tablet? They're on sale now.	還是您想要買台平板？現在平板也有特價喔！
B: Well...I am more of a traditional PC user, so I guess I will just get a desktop.	呃……我是個慣用傳統桌電的人，所以我想我要買台桌電。

A: Just a desktop? We're having a big sale now.A good time to get more!	只要一台桌電嗎？現在大特價喔，是可以多買3C產品的好時機喔！
B: Maybe not…I'm running out of time.	應該不用了……我快沒時間了。

超萬用單字／句型

▸Just let me know...

基本上解釋為「告訴我一聲」。通常用於告訴別人「如果需要幫忙的話，就儘管開口吧」。也可以當作想要別人告知自己事情的發展或進度時用的一句近似拜託的語氣。

❶ **A: Just let me know if you need a ride, ok?**
→ 如果需要我載你一程的話，跟我說一聲就行了。
B: Thank you so much! → 真是太謝謝你了！

❷ **A: Just let me know how things work out.**
→ 記得告訴我一聲接下來怎麼樣了。
B: Yes, I will keep you updated.
→ 好的，我會讓你知道最新的情況。

▸If you need anything,...

這句基本上解釋為「如果你有任何需要。」是一句善意的回應，用來表示如果他人有需要幫忙的話，自己很樂意效勞之意。也可以解釋為「有任何需要的話，就告訴我一聲！」，告訴對方不用客氣的意思。

❶ **A: If you need anything, just let me know, I am just downstairs.**
→ 如果你有任何需要就告訴我一聲，我就在樓下。
B: Thank you! → 謝謝你！

❷ **A: If you need anything, don't hesitate to say it.**
→ 如果需要幫忙，別猶豫儘管說。
B: Ok, got it. → 好的，明白了。

實用句型大補帖

1 **Here's the new iphone! I've been waiting for it to come out for so long!**
是新 iphone 呢！我等它推出好久了！

2 **A desktop has more capabilities, but if you run around a lot, I would suggest a laptop which suits you more.**
桌上型的有較多功能，但如果您常四處奔走的話，我建議筆記型電腦會比較適合您。

3 **Are you looking for any specific models or functions?**
你有在找任何特定的機型或是功能嗎？

4 **I think I'd better get a new digital camera. Mine is too old and the quality of the pictures isn't very good, I guess it is because the number of pixels is too low.**
我想我該買台新的數位相機了。我的太舊了而且畫質不太好。我想是因為像素太低了。

5 **Do you use an iPhone? I know that many people have one, but I think it is quite expensive and they come out with new models too quickly.**
你有在用iPhone嗎？我知道很多人都有，不過我覺得它太貴了而且汰換得太快。

6 **I am more of a traditional PC user, so I am not really fond of the iPad. But if you are a tablet lover, you should definitely try it.**
我是一個比較習慣用傳統桌上型電腦的人，所以我對iPad不是那麼感興趣。不過如果你是平板電腦的愛好者，你絕對要試試看。

7 **I think I need to get a GPS for my car, because I get lost easily. I believe it will be helpful when I drive.**
我想我需要替我的車裝一台衛星導航系統，因為我很容易迷路。我相信它在我開車時會很有幫助。

8 **Why don't you get an iPod? It can store more files and it has more functions compared to the old mp3s. And it looks cooler, too.**
你怎麼不考慮買台iPod？它可以儲存更多檔案而且功能也比舊型mp3多。再者它看起來也比較新潮。

Unit 6

Supermarket

——超市——

和每個人都聊得來 *Track 013*

加粗底線字：詳見「超萬用單字／句型」

A: Welcome to Tal-mart. Please deposit your bag at the checkroom first.	歡迎蒞臨投爾瑪超市，請在寄存處寄放您的包包。
B: How do I get to the checkroom then?	我要怎麼去寄存處呢？
A: It's right there, behind the Lost and Found counter.	在那邊，在失物招領處後面。
B: Thanks!	謝謝！
(After depositing the bag)	（寄存包包後）
B: Excuse me, where can I get a cart?	不好意思，推車在哪裡？
A: They are at the right side of the entrance. Just go straight; you'll see them.	推車在入口處右邊。直走，你就會看到。
B: Thank you.	謝謝！
(After finding the groceries he needs)	（在找齊所有必需生活雜貨後）
B: Excuse me, **where do I pay?**	不好意思，請問到哪結帳？

A: Follow the yellow sign over there, see? And you'll see the cashier.	跟隨黃色標示，在那裡，看到沒？然後你就會看到收銀台。
B: Thanks a lot!	感激不盡！
(At the cashier)	（在收銀台）
A: It's final clear out now, **buy two and get one free**. Want one more bottle of milk?	現在是清倉大拍賣，買二送一。要再來一瓶牛奶嗎？

超萬用單字／句型

▸ Where do I pay?

此句通常用於大型商場、超市及購物廣場，顧客向超市服務人員詢問結帳處或者收銀台的固定用法，意為「到哪結帳？」，相同意義的表達方式還有「where is the cashier?」。

❶ **A: Excuse me, where do I pay?** → 打擾了，請問到哪付款呢？

B: Go along this aisle, and then turn left. You will see the counter.
→ 沿著這條走道一直走，然後向左轉，你就會看到櫃檯。

❷ **A: Can you tell me where the cashier is?**
→ 您能告訴我收銀台在哪嗎？

B: The cashier is just by the food counter.
→ 收銀台就在食品專櫃旁邊。

▸ buy two and get one free

此句一般出現於超市及大型購物商場，是上述盈利機構為了促銷而降價的行銷方式，意為「買二送一」，固定說法為「buy...get...free」。

❶ **A: Buy three and get one free. Miss, do you want to buy some?**
→ 買三送一，小姐要買一些嗎？

B: Ok, give me three kilos. → 好，我買三公斤。

❷ **A: The goods in the supermarket are on sale. Would you want to buy some?** → 超市的商品在促銷，你想買一些嗎？

B: Buy two and get one free? → 是買二送一嗎？

實用句型大補帖

1 **We need to buy some plastic bags. Would you please tell me which aisle the plastic bags are in?**
我們要買些塑膠袋，能告訴我們塑膠袋在哪一條走道嗎？

2 **There is a promotion going on.**
現在有促銷。

3 **Cash or card?**
現金還是刷卡？

4 **Excuse me? Where is the Lost and Found counter?**
打擾一下，請問失物招領處在哪？

5 **Please swipe your card here.**
請在這刷卡。

6 **Please deposit your bags at the checkroom.**
請在寄存處寄放您的包包。

7 **Welcome to Wal-mart, do you need a basket or a cart?**
歡迎光臨沃爾瑪超市，您需要購物籃或者購物車嗎？

8 **The reason I refused to accept your refund is that you have no receipt.**
我之所以不接受您的退貨是因為您沒有發票。

9 **Where do I pay?**
到哪裡結帳呢？

10 **The canned foods are out of stock . Why not choose some frozen foods?**
罐頭食品已銷售一空，為什麼不挑選一些冷凍食品呢？

11 **The supermarket has a final clear out this weekend, buy wo and get one free.**
超市週末要舉行清倉大拍賣，買二送一。

hello!
hi!

Part 4

餐廳用餐，

用餐大小事都
能對任何人清楚說！

Unit 1

Reservation

——訂位——

和每個人都聊得來 *Track 014*

加粗底線字：詳見「超萬用單字／句型」

A: Mariano Italian Cuisine, may I help you?	馬利安諾義大利餐廳，有什麼可以為您服務的嗎？
B: My last name is Cooper. **I want a table for** 7 o'clock this evening.	我姓庫柏，想要預訂今晚7點的位子。
A: May I know how many people will be there?	請問有幾位要用餐呢？
B: I'd like a table for four. But one will come a little later than 7.	我想預訂一張4人桌。其中一個人會晚於7點到。
A: Shall we serve the meal for the three people who come first?	是否要為先抵達的3個人先上餐點呢？
B: No, serve the meal later when everyone has arrived.	不用，等所有人都到再上餐點。
A: Ok. We'll take care of that, Mr. Cooper.	Ok，庫柏先生。我們會留意這一部份的。
B: By the way, **can we dress informally?**	對了，請問我們能穿得隨性一點嗎？
A: I'm afraid not. Our restaurant has a dress code.	我想沒辦法耶。我們餐廳有衣著要求。
B: Oh…Fine.	噢……好吧。

A: We will hold the table for you for 15 minutes. We are looking forward to seeing you on time.	您的訂位將保留15分鐘，我們恭候您的到來。

超萬用單字／句型

▶ I want a table for...

句型「I want a table for...」意為「我想要預訂……位子」，常用於打電話到餐廳預定位子，是訂位的常用語。

❶ **A: Hello, Regent Hotel, may I help you?**
→ 您好，晶華酒店，我能為你服務嗎？
B: I want a table for two people this afternoon.
→ 我想要預定今天下午的二人桌。

❷ **A: I want a table for three people this evening.**
→ 我想要預訂今晚的三人桌。
B: OK, may I have your name please?
→ 好的，能告訴我你的名字嗎？

▶ Can I dress informally?

此句通常用於準備前往餐廳用餐或者受邀到國外友人家中赴宴時，詢問對方對顧客或賓客在服裝上有無要求，意為「我能穿得隨意點嗎？」。受邀出席對方的宴會時一定要問清楚著便裝還是正式服裝，否則比較容易會鬧出笑話。上面所學的超實用單字例句，現在教你用在更多地方！

❶ **A: Hi, Lucy. This is Mary. I want to invite you to attend my birthday party this Sunday.**
→ 露西你好，我是瑪麗。我邀請你本週日參加我的生日派對。
B: OK, but can I dress informally?
→ 好的，但是我能穿得隨性一點嗎？

❷ **A: Does your hotel have any dress code? Can I dress informally?** → 你們旅館有衣著要求嗎？請問我能穿得隨性一點嗎？
B: Of course, you can wear whatever you want.
→ 當然可以，你可以穿任何你想穿的（請隨性）。

實用句型大補帖

1 I'd like to have some information about your meals. What kind of food do you serve?
我想瞭解一下你們餐點資訊。你們提供哪些菜色呢？

2 What are your dinner hours?
你們餐廳晚餐的時間是？

3 I want a table for six o'clock this evening.
我要預訂今晚6點的位子。

4 Does your restaurant have a dress code ?
你們餐廳有衣著要求嗎？

5 When will you come?
您什麼時候會到？

6 We'll take care of that, sir.
我們會留意的，先生。

7 How many people will be there?
請問你們有多少人要來用餐？

8 Would you like the smoking area or the non-smoking area?
你要訂吸煙區的還是非吸煙區呢？

9 We serve a great variety of popular Japanese dishes.
我們餐廳提供各式各樣的日本人氣料理。

10 Can I dress informally?
我能穿得隨性一些嗎？

11 I am only too glad to help you.
我很高興能幫助您。

12 Do you have a cover charge?
請問有收服務費嗎？

13 We will hold the table for you for 15 minutes. We are looking forward to seeing you on time.
餐廳的訂位將會保留15分鐘，我們恭候您的到來。

Unit 2

Order

——點菜——

和每個人都聊得來 Track 015

加粗底線字：詳見「超萬用單字／句型」

A: Hi, I have reserved a table for four for 7 o'clock. My last name is Cooper.	您好，我預約了七點四個人的位子。我姓庫柏。
B: Mr. Cooper, please come this way. I'll show you your table.	庫柏先生，請這邊走。我帶你們到您的位子。
(5 minutes later…)	（五分鐘後……）
B: Sir, are you ready to order now?	先生，你們準備好要點餐了嗎？
A: I have no idea, would you give us some suggestions?	我不知道耶，可以給我們一點建議嗎？
B: My pleasure. Steak is our specialty, and Fillet is the most popular one, especially. The Chefs recommended Fillet.	我很樂意。今日特餐是牛排，尤其是菲力牛排特別受歡迎，廚師們很推薦喔。
A: Oh…then four of this.	好，那就來四客吧。
B: **How would you like your steak?**	您的牛排要幾分熟？

A: One medium-rare, two medium, and one medium-well.	一個三分，兩個五分，一個七分。
B: Ok. The steak you ordered will be served in 7 minutes. **Enjoy** your meal!	好的，您點的牛排7分鐘後就會上桌囉。祝您用餐愉快！

超萬用單字／句型

▸ How would you like your steak?

牛排是西餐廳的「家常菜」，分為一分熟（rare）、三分熟（medium-rare）、五分熟（medium）、七分熟（medium-well）和全熟（well-done）五種。一般在西餐廳點牛排時，服務生會問顧客 How would you like your steak? 意思是您的牛排要幾分熟？如：

❶ **A: How would you like your steak?** → 您的牛排要幾分熟？
B: Well done. → 全熟。

❷ **A: How do you want your steak, medium or well-done?**
→ 您的牛排要幾分熟，五分熟還是全熟？
B: Medium. → 五分熟。

▸ Enjoy+ N / V-ing

一般出現於飯店、餐廳等服務行業，或者也用於主人在家裡招待客人，表示祝福的客套語。如：

❶ **A: Enjoy your trip!** → 祝您旅途愉快！
B: Thank you! → 謝謝。

❷ **A: Enjoy yourself.** → 請好好享受。
B: OK, thanks. → 好的，謝謝。

實用句型大補帖

1 **Are you ready to order?**
您準備好點餐了嗎？

2 **Hi, waiter, could I have the menu, please?**
嗨，服務生，能幫我拿菜單嗎？

3 **What kind of soup would you like?**
您喜歡什麼湯？

4 **How would you like your steak?**
您的牛排要幾分熟？

5 **Enjoy your meal!**
祝您用餐愉快！

6 **Please come this way. I will show you your table .**
請跟我來，我帶您到您的餐桌。

7 **Roasted duck is the specialty of our restaurant. Would you like to have some?**
烤鴨是我們飯店的拿手菜，您要試試看嗎？

8 **We serve Sichuan cuisine and Cantonese cuisine.**
我們有四川菜和廣東菜。

9 **I like spicy food. Would you give me some suggestions?**
我喜歡辣的菜，能幫我推薦嗎?

10 **How about the eggplant? It's our chef's recommendation.**
茄子怎麼樣？這道菜是我們主廚的拿手好菜。

11 **I think Sichuan cuisine is too spicy for me. I should order something else.**
我覺得川菜對我來說太辣了，我應該改點別道菜。

12 **Only with a long trip can you expect to have an authentic dinner.**
惟有經歷長途跋涉，你才會期待吃到道地的晚餐。

13 **Do you want to have some traditional food?**
你想來點當地的傳統小吃嗎？

Unit 3

Bill

──買單──

和每個人都聊得來 Track 016

加粗底線字：詳見「超萬用單字／句型」

A: Don't worry about the bill. Dinner's on me today.	別擔心帳單。今天我請客。
B: Oh! Thanks a bunch! **Do you mind** if I pay for the tip?	噢！太感謝了！你會介意我付小費嗎？
A: Of course not! I think the meal is great and the waiter today served us well.	當然不會啊！我覺得餐點好吃、服務生也服務良好。
B: Yeah…that's why I want to tip him more.	對啊……這就是為什麼我想給他多一點小費。
(At the counter…)	（在櫃台……）
A: I would like to pay for table 18.	我想付18桌的帳單。
B: Do you want to pay with cash or credit card?	您要用現金還是信用卡支付呢？
A: With card.	用卡。
B: It's 65.5 dollars in total.	總共是65.5元。

A: Here's the card and the tip for Terry. He really did a wonderful job!	這是信用卡和給泰瑞的小費。他真的服務得很棒！
B: Thank you for praising our restaurant and my service, Mr. Cooper, **the pleasure is mine**.	感謝您對我們餐廳和我的服務的讚美，庫柏先生。這是我的榮幸。

超萬用單字／句型

▸ The pleasure is mine.

外國人在口語對話上常常會遇到當對方感謝你時，自己也會需要謙遜的回答「這也是我的榮幸」。用法如：

❶ **A: I don't know how to thank you for saving my company!**
→ 我實在不知如何感謝你救了我的公司。
B: Never mind. The pleasure is mine! → 別在意，是我的榮幸！

❷ **A: Thank you for coming to my birthday party today!**
→ 謝謝你今天來我的生日派對！
B: The pleasure is mine! → 是我的榮幸啊！

▸ Do you mind?

外國人在講話時有時候會停下來徵詢對方意見，看對方同意或不同意自己的作法，如：

❶ **A: I'll drive. Do you mind?** → 我來開車，你介意嗎？
B: Not at all. → 一點也不。

❷ **A: I might need to stay at your place this weekend. Do you mind?** → 我這禮拜可能需要住你家，你介意嗎？
B: Of course not! → 當然不會！

實用句型大補帖

1 **Excuse me, the sandwich and blueberry juice cost me a hundred dollars. How much is the juice?**
不好意思，我的三明治跟藍莓汁要價一百元。那果汁一瓶多少？

2 **I think the waiter today served us well! We should tip him more!**
我覺得今天的服務生服務得很好！我們應該給他多一點小費！

3 **Jimmy and Sarah had an argument at the restaurant counter last night. They couldn't compromise on how much tip they should leave for the restaurant.**
吉米和莎拉昨晚在餐廳櫃檯爭吵。他們對於要留給餐廳多少小費無法達成共識。

4 **I suppose that the Chinese restaurant would charge less compared to the French restaurant.**
我猜中式餐廳和法式餐廳比應該會比較便宜。

5 **Thank you for praising my restaurant and service, Ms. Lu, the pleasure is mine.**
盧小姐，感謝您稱讚本餐廳以及服務，這實在是我的榮幸！

6 **Do you mind if I take several name cards of your restaurant and give them away to my friends?**
你介意我拿一些你們餐廳的名片給我朋友嗎？

7 **The waiter didn't clean up our table before we sat, which is why I need to see the manager now to complain about it.**
我們入座前服務生並未清理我們的桌子，這也是為什麼我現在必須要見經理並抱怨這件事。

Unit 4

Bar

——酒吧——

和每個人都聊得來 *Track 017*

加粗底線字：詳見「超萬用單字／句型」

A: Kate looks down these days, why don't we ask her to have some fun with us tonight?	凱特最近看起來心情很低落，要不要今晚找她一起狂歡？
B: Yep! Nice idea! I happen to know a great bar nearby!	好！好主意！我剛好知道這附近有間很讚的酒吧！
A: Hey, Kate! I remember you told me you're fond of tequila, right? I know a bar which serves the best Margarita!	嗨，凱特！我記得妳説過妳超愛龍舌蘭酒，對嗎？ 我知道有家酒吧的瑪格麗塔超讚！
B: Really? When are you going there? Count me in then!	真的嗎？妳們什麼時候要去？加我一個！
A: Sure! It's just nearby; we'll go there tonight. Let's go!	當然囉！酒吧就在附近，我們今晚就會去。一起去吧！
(At the bar nearby…)	（在附近的酒吧……）
B: **Frankly speaking,** the Margarita here is super fantastic! I love it!	老實説，這間的瑪格麗塔真是讚上加讚耶！我超愛！
A: I'll say.	我就説吧！
B: Oh! **I am in the mood for** liquor now! I will have cherry blossom beer next!	噢！我現在很有喝酒的興致！下一杯要喝櫻花啤酒！

A: Holy Moly! Kate, I really don't think you can hold your liquor...I highly suggest that we go home right now!	天啊！凱特，我真的不覺得妳酒量ok……我建議我們現在就回家！
B: Since we're already here, just let your hair down!	我們都來了，就放鬆然後好好玩嘛！

超萬用單字／句型

▸ Frankly speaking, ...

Frank 在這裡是坦白的意思，當外國人想表達內心真正的想法時，通常會以這類句型開頭，如：

❶ **A: This jacket looks cool! How about I buy one for my boyfriend?** → 這件夾克看起來好酷！你覺得我買一件給我男友怎麼樣？

B: Frankly speaking, I don't think it will look good on your boyfriend. → 老實說，我不覺得妳男友穿這件會好看。

❷ **A: This purse is too tiny, and the color is not pretty. What's worse is the price is unreasonable.**

→ 這個錢包太小了，而且顏色也不漂亮，更糟的是價錢很不合理。

B: Frankly speaking, you are too picky. → 老實說，妳太挑剔了。

▸ I'm in the mood for...

外國人常以此句表達「有做某事的心情」，如：

❶ **A: Hey! I'm going to buy some beverages. Do you want me to buy something for you?**

→ 嘿！我正要去買些飲料，要我幫你買點什麼嗎？

B: Sure, I'm in the mood for a cup of coffee, thank you.

→ 當然好，我正想喝杯咖啡，謝謝你。

❷ **A: Kelly is inviting me to go shopping with her. Do you want to join us?**

→ 凱莉正邀請我一起去逛街。妳要不要一起來？

B: Thank you, but I'm not in the mood for it now.

→ 謝謝妳，但我現在沒有心情逛街。

實用句型大補帖

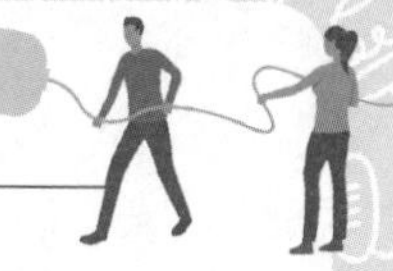

1 **Frankly speaking, I don't care for all sorts of beer because you might get an annoying beer gut.**
老實說，各種啤酒我都不喜歡，因為那讓人有討人厭的啤酒肚。

2 **It seems that Kelly has been in a bad mood for the whole week. How about we invite her to have some fun tonight? I know a nice bar near her apartment.**
凱莉好像已經心情不好整整一個禮拜了。不如我們邀請她去找點樂子吧？我知道她家附近有間不錯的酒吧。

3 **You know what? A little bird told me that the handsome bartender we met last weekend already has someone.**
你知道嗎？有人告訴我說上週末我們遇到的那個帥氣酒保已經有對象了。

4 **I think we can call Kenny a typical alcoholic. He has been drunk every night since breaking up with his girlfriend last year.**
我想我們可以稱肯尼為典型酒鬼了。自從他去年跟女朋友分手後就每晚把自己灌醉。

5 **I'm in the mood for liquor tonight, I'll have a whisky straight.**
我今晚有喝點烈酒的興致，我要一杯純威士忌。

6 **Look over there! The lady bartender is the most beautiful one I've ever seen in Taipei.**
你看那邊！那個女酒保是我在台北看過最美的一個。

7 **Don't you think that a bartender should have better social skills? John is the worst one I've ever met.**
你不覺得一個酒保應該要有好一點的社交技巧嗎？約翰真的是我遇過最糟糕的一個了。

8 **Josh, I remember you've told me you are a big fan of vodka, right? Come and try this, the Bloody Mary here is pretty nice.**
賈許，我記得你跟我說過你超愛伏特加，對吧？來試試這個，這裡的血腥瑪莉很不錯。

9 **I'm in a good mood! The bartender gave me and all of my friends a shot for free!**
我今天心情很好！酒保請我和我所有的朋友一杯免費的酒！

10 **Are you serious? Do you really want to finish all of the cocktails here? You'll vomit later!**
你是認真的嗎？你真的要喝完這邊所有的雞尾酒？等一下你會吐的！

11 **I really don't think you can hold your liquor ...I highly suggest that we go home right now!**
我真的不覺得你酒量ok……我建議我們現在就回家！

Part 5

美髮美體，

在國外美容隨時
都能開口用英文聊！

Unit 1

Hairstyle

——美髮——

和每個人都聊得來 Track 018

加粗底線字：詳見「超萬用單字／句型」

A: Rita, you changed your hairstyle? Wow, it really looks excellent on you!	瑞塔，妳換髮型了嗎？哇，妳的髮型跟妳很搭耶！
B: I just got a hair-cut and dyed my hair in light brown.	我剛剪短頭髮然後把頭髮染成淺棕色。
A: The color fits your skin color! Gorgeous! Really makes you a lady!	這個顏色和妳的膚色很搭！很讚！妳看起來就是個名媛！
B: Oh…I really love this color! I can't stop talking about the process of the hair-cut…Oh…the stylist was just so charming!	噢……我愛死這個顏色了！我沒辦法不談我剪髮的過程……噢……設計師超迷人的！
(half an hour later…)	（半小時後……）
A: You know…You must go to that hair salon, and appoint that stylist to change a better hairstyle…	妳知道嗎？妳該去那家髮型店，然後指定那個設計師，再剪一個更美的髮型……
B: Oh…Cut it out! You've talked about this topic for 30 minutes! **Give me a break!**	噢……妳可以停了吧！妳已經談這個話題半小時了！饒了我吧！
A: Hey! **Let's put it this way**, you really should go to that hair salon and get a new and chic hairstyle!	嘿！那我這樣說吧，妳真的該去那家髮型店換個今年最時尚的髮型！

B: Come on! You didn't say it only for my sake, right?	拜託！妳不是只為了我好才說這種話的，對吧？
A: Yeah…I want to see that stylist again, but I also want you to look nice…	是啦……我想再見那個設計師一次，但也想要妳看起來很棒啊……

超萬用單字／句型

▶ Give me a break!

外國人在口語對話上常用，當想拒絕別人無厘頭的要求或是請求時，就可以派上用場，其意思近似中文的「放過我吧！」及「讓我休息一下吧」，用法如：

❶ **A: Will you please help me finish my English project?**
→ 你能不能幫我完成我的英文報告？
B: Oh! Give me a break! → 噢，讓我休息一下吧！

❷ **A: Will you please wash the dishes for me?**
→ 你能不能幫我洗盤子？
B: Oh, I just finished cleaning the bathroom! Give me a break! → 我才剛清完浴室，饒了我吧！

▶ Let's put it this way

外國人在口語對話上有的時候怕對方可能會不瞭解自己的意思，因此常常會進行所謂的「換句話說」，其意思同於中文所說的「我這樣說好了」，來闡揚自己語意，其用法如：

❶ **A: What do you mean by saying that she is a fat lazy pig?**
→ 你說她是隻大懶豬是什麼意思？
B: Let's put it this way, she wakes up at 11:00 every day and eat five meals a day!
→ 我這樣說好了，她每天都十一點才起床且一天吃五餐！

❷ **A: What do you mean by calling him a fox?**
→ 你叫他狐狸是什麼意思？
B: Let's put it this way, he is cunning sometimes.
→ 這麼說好了，他有時很狡猾。

實用句型大補帖

1 **Julia, when did you dye your hair? I like the new color!**

茱麗亞，妳什麼時候染頭髮的？我喜歡這顏色！

2 **Lisa, how do you want your hair dyed? Light brown or dark brown?**

麗莎，妳希望妳的頭髮染成怎樣？淺褐色還是深褐色？

3 **I guess Clara got a perm last week. That's why it looks so curly.**

我猜克拉拉上禮拜去燙頭髮了！難怪看起來這麼捲。

4 **Is it O.K. if I use some of your hairspray?**

你介意我用一些你的髮膠嗎？

5 **Jamie cut her hair really short this semester and was accidentally recognized as a boy by our history teacher.**

潔咪這學期把頭髮剪得超短然後被我們歷史老師誤認為是男生。

6 **Mom, would you help me dye my hair brown? I'm sick of being a blonde all the time!**

媽，妳能不能幫我把頭髮染成褐色？我厭倦了總是當金髮女郎！

7 **I'd like to cut my fringe short, please.**

我想剪短瀏海，麻煩你了！

8 **Your hair is just too short to get a perm.**

你的頭髮實在太短以致於無法燙髮。

Unit 2

Skincare

——護膚——

和每個人都聊得來 Track 019

加粗底線字：詳見「超萬用單字／句型」

A: Welcome to Dream Skin-care Center. May I help you?	歡迎來到夢想護膚中心！我能為您做什麼服務？
B: Could you recommend your body care services?	可以請你推薦你們的美體療程嗎？
A: Which part of the body would you like to take care of?	您想護理身體哪個部位呢？
B: I heard this skin-care center is renowned for your skin-care expertise. Would you tell me which skin-care service I need now?	我聽說你們中心是首屈一指的護膚專門店。可以請你告訴我我需要哪種美體療程嗎？
A: Well...Do you apply lotion or other skin-care products every day?	嗯……請問您每天都有擦乳液或保養品嗎？
B: Not exactly. I seldom use those skin-care products.	不太擦耶。我很少用保養品。
A: Then I suggest that you take our full-body deep skin care. The skin care service can moisturize the dry skin of your whole body.	那我建議您購買全身深層美體護膚療程。這個護膚療程可以滋潤您乾燥的全身肌膚。
B: **What is the price like?**	價位大概多少呢？

A: It is about 200 dollars. You can also have an essential oil massage at the price of only 30 dollars!	大約200元，您可以以優惠價30元搭配精油按摩喔！
B: Oh…sounds great! I will take both… **Oops!** I forgot my purse!	噢……聽起來很棒呢！我想要購買這兩個療程……唉呀！我忘了帶錢包了！

超萬用單字／句型

▶ Oops!

是歐美人士常說的六大經典語氣詞之一，意為「哦 / 哎呀……」，表示感嘆，通常用在說話人意識到自己犯了錯的情況下，有些化解尷尬的語氣。

❶ **A: Oops! I forgot today is your birthday.**

→ 哎呀，我忘記了今天是你的生日。

B: Give me a beautiful gift, or I will never forgive you.

→ 給我漂亮的禮物，否則我永遠不原諒你。

❷ **A: Do you know where my dog is?** → 你們知道我的狗在哪裡嗎？

B: Oops! I forgot to let it in. → 糟了，我忘記讓牠進屋了。

▶ What is the price like?

「What is the price like?」是希望知道產品價位範圍的慣用句型。歐美人士通常用於第一次詢價時。

❶ **A: What a piano! What is the price like?**

→ 真是台好鋼琴！價位多少？

B: It's between 15,000 to 16,000 dollars.

→ 在 15,000 至 16,000 之間。

❷ **A: I want to do colorful French Acrylic Nails.**

→ 我想做彩色的法式水晶指甲。

B: Must be expensive! What are the prices like?

→ 應該很貴吧？價位大概多少呢？

實用句型大補帖

1 **I'm wondering if you do body care.**
你們有全身護理服務嗎？

2 **Could you recommend some services that are around $5,000?**
你能推薦我價位大約5000元的服務嗎？

3 **Which part of the body would you like to be taken care of?**
您想護理身體的哪一部位呢？

4 **I heard that you are an expert in skin care.**
我聽說您是肌膚護理方面的專家。

5 **There are always some pimples on my face. How can I get rid of them?**
我的臉上總是有些痘痘，怎麼才能去除它們呢？

6 **Later, I will apply the lavender oil to wipe out pore-clogging dirt and oil.**
接下來我將會用薰衣草精油去除毛孔污垢和油脂。

7 **Oops! I poured too much lotion out.**
哦！我不小心倒太多乳液了！

8 **I apply a light moisturizer in the morning with sunscreen to protect my skin for the day.**
我每天早上都會擦些保濕和防曬霜來保護我的肌膚。

9 **The skin care in our beauty salon helps you look younger.**
我們美容院的皮膚護理讓你看起來更年輕。

10 **Go to bed earlier and you will stay younger.**
早點睡，然後你就可常保年輕。

Unit 3

Body Spa

——美體——

和每個人都聊得來 Track 020

加粗底線字：詳見「超萬用單字／句型」

A: After working for 10 hours without any relaxation, I am totally stressed out.	在連續工作10小時沒有休息後，我真的壓力超大的。
B: Why don't we go to have a spa in this **Indian Summer**?	我們為何不在這個秋高氣爽的好日子spa一下？
A: Yeah! Let's go! By the way, **how often** do you go to the spa center?	好耶！走吧！對了，妳很常去spa嗎？
B: I am a big fan of spas, so I go twice or three times a week.	我是spa迷，所以我每週固定去個一、兩次。
(In the spa center…)	（在spa中心裡……）
A: Welcome. Is there anything I can do for you?	歡迎，有什麼能為兩位服務的嗎？
B: Oh, my friend has been working for 10 hours straight. Can you give her a full-body massage?	噢，我朋友連續工作了10小時，妳們可以替她做全身按摩嗎？
A: How about you? Do you want to try a Thai massage? As a VIP member, you can get a free "rosemary facial steam" with Thai massage.	那您呢？您要試試泰式按摩嗎？身為VIP會員，您做泰式按摩的話，可以免費做「迷迭香蒸臉」喔！

B: I've caught a cold. So, I think I need a customized program.	我剛得了感冒。我想我需要客製化療程。
A: Ok, I will arrange the massage programs for you two. Please wait a moment and have some warm herbal tea.	好的，將為兩位安排按摩療程。請稍等一下、喝杯溫香草茶。
B: Thank you.	謝謝！

超萬用單字／句型

▶ How often...

how often：多常、多久一次（對頻率副詞提問），通常要用頻率副詞或諸如 every day, each week, once a week, twice a day, four times a month 等來回答。

❶ **A: How often did he go to visit his parents?**
→ 他多久去看一次他的父母？
B: I don't quite know, maybe about once a week.
→ 我也不太清楚，大概一週一次吧！

❷ **A: How often do you send a letter to her?**
→ 你多久寫信給她一次？
B: I send a letter to her every day. → 我每天都寫信給她。

▶ Indian Summer

India Summer 並不是「印度的夏天」的意思，而是歐美國家用以形容深秋比較暖和的一段日子，一般出現在 9 月下旬、10 月和 11 月，有時候也會出現在 8 月或 12 月。

❶ **A: Would you like to go out with me in the Indian Summer?**
→ 你願意在這秋高氣爽的日子裡和我一同出遊嗎？
B: Of course, I like the sunshine. → 當然了，我很喜歡陽光。

❷ **A: My family will go for an outing in the Indian Summer.**
→ 我們家打算在深秋暖和的日子去郊遊。
B: It's really a good idea. Can I join you?
→ 這真是個不錯的想法，我能加入你們嗎？

實用句型大補帖

1 **Why not try a Thai massage? The masseuse will customize a training program for you.**
為什麼不試試泰式按摩呢? 女按摩師會為你量身訂做訓練計畫。

2 **Will you do the "rosemary and rose petal facial steam" for me?**
你們能幫我做個「迷迭香和玫瑰花瓣蒸臉」嗎？

3 **Is there anything I can help you with?**
有什麼我可以幫忙的嗎？

4 **On which part of your body?**
在您身體的哪個部位呢？

5 **I caught a cold. Can you give me a full-body massage?**
我感冒了，你能給我做個全身按摩嗎？

6 **What should I do to cut down on my weight?**
我怎麼做才能減輕體重呢?

7 **Your body is full of toxins. Let's try to clear it away .**
你的身體充滿了毒素。我們試著排除它吧。

8 **Why don't you go out to have a spa in the Indian Summer?**
為什麼不在這秋高氣爽的季節去體驗spa？

9 **Please relax. I will be massaging your back now.**
請放輕鬆，我要開始按摩你的背了。

10 **What can you do about my large pores?**
你有什麼辦法改善我的毛孔粗大呢？

Part 6

談情說愛，

國籍不是問題、
外國男／女友手到擒來！

Unit 1

Flirting

——曖昧——

和每個人都聊得來 Track 021

加粗底線字：詳見「超萬用單字／句型」

A: Hi, Carol. What are you doing?	嗨，卡蘿。妳在做什麼？
B: I'm texting Jason now.	我在傳訊息給傑森。
A: Jason Booker? The leader of the football team? I thought he's seeing someone now.	傑森．布克爾？足球隊隊長？我以為他一直都有女朋友。
B: Not really. He**'s available** now! Haven't you heard the rumor?	也不是這樣。他現在沒有女朋友啦！妳還沒聽到傳聞嗎？
A: Uh...So last Wednesday, when you told me on the phone that you were on a date, were you with him?	呃……所以上禮拜三妳電話裡説在約會，妳是跟他嗎？
B: Yeah...hey! don't look at me as if I were something!	對啊……嘿！別用奇怪的眼光看我喔！
A: Sweet Jesus! You are dating the **Mr. Right** of all the girls in the whole school?	天啊！妳跟全校女生的夢中情人約會？
B: Correct! I've been fascinated by him lately!	對啊！我想我最近對他著迷了！

A: Don't be silly! Girls like us wouldn't easily catch his eye...	別傻了！像我們這種女生他不會放在心上的……
B: Well...then how do you explain what he has done for me these days?	嗯……那妳要怎麼解釋最近他為我做的這些事呢？

超萬用單字／句型

▸ Mr. Right

意為「白馬王子、真命天子」，從字面上理解就是合適先生，引申為合適的人，因為在西方人觀念裡談戀愛或者婚嫁，合適最重要。這個人不是簡單的男朋友，應該是指能給自己一個感情穩定歸宿的人，一般人是認為將來可以結婚的人，也有認為是可以白頭到老的人。

❶ **A: Have you found your Mr. Right?** → 找到你的白馬王子了嗎？
B: Not yet. I'm too picky to find anyone that suits me.
→ 還沒有，我太挑剔以至於很難找到適合我的人。

❷ **A: Where is my Mr. Right?** → 我的真命天子在哪裡？
B: Maybe the guy in front of you is your sweetie.
→ 或許你前面的這傢伙就會是你的心上人呢。

▸ Are you available?

此句話的意思為「你現在有空嗎？」，但學英語切忌不分語境和望文生義，因此，如果語境不同，就表示老外在委婉的詢問你「是不是單身、有沒有可能和他約會、有沒有機會追求你」。

❶ **A: Are you available tonight?** → 今晚有空嗎？
B: Sorry, have we been introduced? → 不好意思，我們認識嗎？

❷ **A: May I ask you a personal question? Are you available?**
→ 我能冒昧的問您一個私人問題嗎？請問您單身嗎？
B: Yeah, I'm single. → 是，我單身。

實用句型大補帖

1 **If you don't mind me saying so, I have never done so much for anyone.**
如果你不介意我這樣說的話，我從來沒有為一個人付出如此多。

2 **Your smile is so charming.**
你的笑容很迷人。

3 **What do you think of me?**
你覺得我怎麼樣？

4 **If I may ask, are you single now?**
我冒昧的問一下，你單身嗎？

5 **Are you available?**
你單身嗎？/你有空嗎？

6 **I've had a crush on you at first sight.**
我對你一見鍾情。

7 **Do you remember that this is the place where we first met? I hope I can have a date with you here again.**
你記得這是我們初次見面的地方嗎？我希望能夠以後能再和你在這裡約會。

8 **I like everything about him.**
我喜歡他的一切。

9 **It was not until today that I realized that you are important to me.**
直到今天我才意識到你對我來說很重要。

10 **To each his/her own .**
各有所好。

11 **You know, you caught my eye when we first met.**
你知道嗎，初次見面時我就被你吸引了。

Unit 2

In Love

——熱戀——

和每個人都聊得來 Track 022

加粗底線字：詳見「超萬用單字／句型」

A: Carol looks like she is floating on cloud nine. What's wrong with her?	卡蘿看起來心情很好，她是怎樣？
B: Haven't you heard about it?	你還沒聽說嗎？
B: What? I only heard about how Mr. Shelvan will flunk you if you keep skipping his class.	聽說什麼？我只聽說如果一直翹希爾萬老師的課，會被他當掉。
A: Hey! Do you want to know rumors about Carol or not?	欸！你到底要不要聽卡蘿的傳言啊？
B: Oh, my fault. Shoot it, I am all ears now!	喔，抱歉。講吧，我聽。
A: Do you know that Jason has just ended his **puppy love**?	你知道傑森剛跟他初戀分手了嗎？
B: What? You mean our sweet Jason has broken up with his "true love", Chloe?	啊？你是說好好先生傑森跟他的「真愛」克洛伊分手了嗎？
A: Exactly! What's worse, he **is all over** Carol now.	沒錯！更慘的是他現在愛卡蘿愛得要死。

B: No way! Carol Davidson? That nerdy and shy Carol?	不會吧！卡蘿．大衛森嗎？那個害羞的書呆子卡蘿嗎？
A: That's not a joke. Now our little Carol steals the whole show!	沒在跟你開玩笑，現在小卡蘿成為萬眾矚目的焦點了！

超萬用單字／句型

▸ be all over sb.

有別於 over 在英文中有著結束的含義，歐美人士在使用「be all over sb.」通常兩層含義：1. 為之著迷，討好；2. 黏著 / 纏著某人，不給某人空間。

❶ **A: How do you think of Anna and Terry's relationship?**
→ 你怎麼看待安娜和泰瑞的關係？
B: Anna's all over Terry. → 安娜（單方面）迷上泰瑞。

❷ **A: Why does she follow you every time you show up?**
→ 她為什麼每次你出現就跟著你？
B: She's been all over me since the party last weekend.
→ 從上週派對上她就開始纏著我不放。

▸ puppy love

初戀，在英文裡就是 puppy love 或者 calf love，puppy 意為小狗，calf 意為小牛，有點初生之犢的意思，是指年紀輕輕時的第一次戀愛。

❶ **A: Are you serious? Are you sure that it isn't puppy love.**
→ 你是認真的嗎？你確定這不是初戀？
B: Of course not, I'm already eighteen years old.
→ 當然不是了，我已經十八歲了啊。

❷ **A: Don't be silly, it was just puppy love, Ok?**
→ 別傻了，那只是個初戀而已，好嗎？
B: I know, but I can't forget him. → 我知道，但是我就是忘不了他。

實用句型大補帖

1 **I feel that I've fallen in love with Peter. He is an outstanding guy.**
我覺得我好像愛上彼得了，他是個出色的男生。

2 **How long have you been going out?**
你們交往多久了？

3 **We met at a dance party. It was love at first sight .**
我們在舞會上相識。是一見鍾情。

4 **She/He turns me on .**
她/他讓我眼睛為之一亮。

5 **Are you sure there's a place in your heart for her?**
你確定她在你心裡佔有一席之地嗎？

6 **Let's hitch it. I love you with all my heart.**
讓我們在一起吧！我全心全意愛你。

7 **When he met her, he had feelings for her.**
當他見到她時，就對她愛慕不已。

8 **To the world you may be just one person. To one person you may be the world.**
對於世界，你可能只是一個人，但對於某個人，你卻是整個世界。

9 **No one can imagine how much I love her.**
沒有人知道我有多愛她。

10 **I'll be yours through all the years, till the end of time.**
不論經過多少年我都屬於你，直到永遠。

Unit 3

Argument

——爭執——

和每個人都聊得來 Track 023

加粗底線字：詳見「超萬用單字／句型」

A: Gloria, how can you say that to Virginia? You shouldn't have done that!	葛洛麗雅，妳怎麼可以這樣對維吉妮亞說話？妳真不應該那樣做！
B: What's your problem? Who do you think you are?	你怎麼回事啊？你以為你是誰？
A: Hey, you don't have to talk like this! I'm just giving you my advice.	嘿！別這樣和我說話！我只是在給妳建議。
B: Don't give me your attitude! Leave me alone!	別跟我擺架子！走開！
A: I'm telling you for the last time! Please at least show some respect! I'm your husband, not your enemy.	我最後再告訴妳一次，請表現出妳的尊重！我是妳老公，不是敵人。
B: Yeah, my husband...Just look at what you did when that crazy woman was insulting me!	是啊，我的老公……看看你在那個瘋女人汙辱我的時候都做了些什麼！
A: You've really gone too far! Virginia is not "that crazy woman". She's my sister!	你太過分了！維吉妮亞不是「那個瘋女人」，她是我姐！
B: **Knock it off!** She has hated me since we've been together. I wish I had never met you.	少來這一套，她從我們在一起時就開始討厭我了。我真後悔這輩子遇到你！

A: **Are you crazy?** So, do you want to break up with me?	妳瘋了嗎？所以，要分手嗎？
B: Get over yourself! Let's do it!	別自以為是了！分手吧！

超萬用單字／句型

▶ Are you crazy?

歐美人士在遇到親人、朋友及愛人無理取鬧或者是出現不可理喻的情形時，通常會說「Are you crazy? 你瘋了嗎？」表示無法理解或是一種無奈的情緒，其中尤以美國人最常用。

❶ **A: Why didn't you take my phone call at that time? I needed your help.** → 那時候你為什麼不接電話？我需要你的幫助。

B: Are you crazy? I was at a meeting when you called.
→ 你瘋了嗎？你打來時我正在開會耶。

❷ **A: Are you crazy? You dare to quarrel with your mother?**
→ 你瘋了嗎？你居然敢和你母親吵架？

B: I don't want to either. → 我也不願意阿。

▶ Knock it off!

歐美人士在吵架時要對方停止謾罵會說：「Knock it off!」意指「少來！」，也有「夠了！」、「停止！」的意思。所以當有人大聲說話、唱歌吵到你時，也可以用 Knock it off!

❶ **A: Buy me that purse...It's just made for me!**
→ 幫我買那個包嘛……它根本就是為人家量身訂做的！

B: Knock it off! You've been talking about this the whole morning. → 夠了！妳已經說了一個早上了。

❷ **A: Why not tell me the truth the first time we met?**
→ 你為什麼不在我們第一次見面的時候告訴我真相？

B: Knock it off! You wouldn't have believed me then.
→ 夠了！那時候我說你也不信。

實用句型大補帖

1 **You piss me off. Take a hike!**
你氣死我了。哪裡涼快哪裡去吧。

2 **I'm fed up. I can't take it anymore!**
我厭倦了。我受不了了！

3 **I've had enough of your garbage.**
我聽膩了你的廢話。

4 **You are out of your mind.**
你頭腦有問題！

5 **Don't give me your excuses/ No more excuses.**
別找藉口。

6 **Get off my back.**
少跟我囉嗦。

7 **Don't nag me! I'm not going to put up with this!**
別在我面前嘮叨！我再也不要忍受了！

8 **Nonsense! Enough is enough!**
鬼話！已經夠了！

9 **You asked for it.**
你自找的。

10 **It's none of your business .**
不關你的事。

11 **Let's break up , and get out of my life.**
我們分手吧。從我的生活中消失吧！

12 **Don't push me.**
別逼我。

Unit 4

Reconciliation

——和好——

和每個人都聊得來 Track 024

加粗底線字：詳見「超萬用單字／句型」

A: Gloria, baby, why are you carrying that luggage?	葛洛麗雅，寶貝，妳為什麼提著行李？
B: Well…You just mentioned breaking up…	你剛才提到分手……
A: Dear, I was totally out of my mind. I'm terribly sorry. I didn't mean it.	親愛的，我剛氣瘋了。真的超級抱歉。我不是故意的。
B: Neither do I…I was so pissed off by her… (weeping)	我也不是……我只是被她氣瘋了……（啜泣）
A: I know…I know… Come here. (Hugging her)	我知道……我知道……來吧。（抱住她）
A: You know you're my dear, dear life-long partner. No one's more important than you.	妳知道妳是我的親愛的一輩子的伴侶。沒有人比妳更重要了。
B: Even Virginia? Every time she teases me, you just stand there, saying nothing.	比維吉妮亞更重要？每次她嘲諷我你都只是安靜地站在一邊。
A: Of course. I said nothing because I don't want to hurt Mom.	妳當然比她重要。我不說話是不想傷媽媽的心。
B: Oh… it's all my fault… (weeping) I thought…you're on her side…	噢……是我的錯……（啜泣）我以為……你站在她那邊……

A: Never. I'm yours. The last thing I want is to lose you. **Are you all right** now?	絕對不是。我是妳的，我最不希望的就是失去妳。妳現在有好一點嗎？
B: Yeah…**I beg your pardon** for getting you wrong. I'm yours, too. I love you!	嗯……我請你原諒我，因為我誤會你了。我也是你的，我愛你！

超萬用單字／句型

▶Are you all right?

用法比較廣闊，可用於陌生人、親人、戀人及朋友間，表示經過一段時間的不見面，詢問對方的身體或精神狀況如何，意為「你還好嗎？」。

❶ **A: Are you all right?** → 你一切都好嗎？

B: Yeah, I think so. What about you? → 嗯，我還好，你呢？

❷ **A: Paul, you don't look good. Are you all right?**

→ 保羅，你氣色看起來不大好，你還好吧？

B: I have a stomachache, but what's the most important is I'm very nervous. → 我胃痛，最重要的是我很緊張。

▶I beg your pardon

此句通常用於感到歉意的場合，有兩種含義。其一意為「請你原諒我」，表示自己做錯事後請求對方原諒自己的過失；其二意為「不好意思，請您再說一遍好嗎？」，表示由於沒有聽清楚對方的話而請求對方重複。

❶ **A: I messed up your room, so I beg your pardon.**

→ 我把你的房間弄髒了，請你原諒我。

B: It doesn't matter. Just help me clean it.

→ 沒關係，只要幫我整理好就好。

❷ **A: I beg your pardon?** → 不好意思，您說什麼？

B: I said that you can be a good student if you finish your homework on time. → 我說如果你準時完成回家作業你就是個好學生。

實用句型大補帖

1 **I'm sorry. I didn't mean to hurt you.**
對不起，我不是有意要傷害你的。

2 **I'm sorry I got angry at you at the party.**
我抱歉在派對上對你發飆。

3 **I'm terribly sorry, dear. Are you all right?**
對不起，親愛的。你還好嗎？

4 **I really don't want to lose you. I beg your pardon.**
我真的不想失去你，請你原諒我吧。

5 **I was wrong. I shouldn't have lied to you. I love you forever.**
我錯了。我不該對你說謊。我永遠愛你。

6 **Those days when we were together appear in my mind from time to time. Can you forgive me?**
那些我們在一起的時光不時地浮現在我的腦海。你能原諒我嗎？

7 **I will forgive you, but not next time.**
我會原諒你，但是下不為例。

8 **You are still the person who will be forever in my heart.**
你仍是那個永遠住在我心裡的人。

9 **This flower stands for my eternal love for you.**
這朵花代表我對你永恆的愛。

10 **I only have eyes for you.**
我只想著你。

11 **I will love your family as well as you.**
我會像愛你一樣地愛你的家人。

Unit 5

Proposal

——求婚——

和每個人都聊得來 Track 025

加粗底線字：詳見「超萬用單字／句型」

A: Scarlett! Guess how many years we have been together until today?	史嘉蕾！猜猜到今天我們在一起多久了？
B: Well…What day is today? Oh! It's October 3rd!	嗯……今天是幾月幾號？噢！是10月3號耶！
A: Yeah, today's our anniversary. 5 years! Wanna go somewhere to celebrate?	對啊，是我們交往紀念日喔。5年！想去哪裡慶祝嗎？
B: Wow…I can't imagine that 5 years just passed! Time really flies, right?	哇……我不敢想像5年就這樣過去了！真是時間飛逝，對嗎？
A: Can't agree with you more! I can still recall that scarlet scarf you wore the first day we first met at that café…	我超有同感！我還可以記得我們第一次在那間咖啡廳見面時妳的赤紅圍巾。
B: Oh…I miss that café! What's the name of it? Should we go there again today?	噢……我好懷念那間咖啡廳喔！叫什麼名字？要不要我們今天再去那裡一次？
(At the café…)	（在那間咖啡廳……）
B: Oh! This was where I first saw you! I remember you wore glasses with blue frames and sat here…	噢！就是在這裡我第一次見到你戴著你的藍框眼鏡，坐在這裡……

A: I think it's time to say it to you.	我想是時候對妳說了吧。
B: Say what?	說什麼？
A: Dear Scarlett, You're the one I want to spend the rest of my life with. **Let's tie the knot. Will you marry me?**	親愛的史嘉蕾，妳是我想共度下半輩子的伴侶。我們一起生活吧！嫁給我好嗎？

超萬用單字／句型

▸ Will you marry me?

此句型是非常符合歐美風俗習慣的，求婚表達方式單刀直入、開門見山，意為「你願意嫁給我嗎？ / 你願意娶我嗎？」，相同意義的表達方式還有「Will you be my wife / husband?」

❶ **A: Mary, will you marry me?** → 瑪麗，妳願意嫁給我嗎？
B: Sorry, I still don't think I'm well-prepared for marriage.
→ 不好意思，我想我現在還沒有準備好結婚。

❷ **A: Will you marry me, Paul?** → 保羅，你願意娶我嗎？
B: Of course. You are so beautiful, everyone wants to marry you. → 當然了，你這麼漂亮，每個人都願意娶你。

▸ Let's tie the knot.

此句型是一種較為含蓄且比較有文采的求婚表達方式，多用於比較喜歡咬文嚼字的情侶。意為「讓我們喜結連理吧！」，相同方式的表達方式還有「Let's get hitched! 讓我們成為比翼鳥吧！」

❶ **A: Let's tie the knot.** → 讓我們結為連理吧！
B: Ok, why not? I want to be your wife.
→ 好啊，為什麼不呢？我也想成為你的妻子。

❷ **A: Katarina, let's tie the knot.** → 凱特琳娜，讓我們結為連理吧！
B: Oh, I'm so happy. → 哇，我好幸福。

實用句型大補帖

1 **I want to grow old with you.**
我想和你白頭偕老，共度一生。

2 **I think it's time we took some vows.**
我想是我們該許下誓言的時候了。

3 **I think it's time we settle down .**
我想是我們該穩定下來的時候了。

4 **I want to spend the rest of my life with you.**
我要與你共度餘生。

5 **Will you be my wife?**
你願意成為我的妻子嗎？

6 **I don't want to get married yet.**
我還不想結婚。

7 **Putting on this ring means that I want to be your wife.**
戴上這枚戒指，表示我願意成為你的妻子。

8 **I think we should get engaged first.**
我覺得我們應該先訂婚。

9 **I've got ready for a life-long commitment.**
我已經為一輩子的承諾準備好了。

10 **I want to be with you forever.**
我想與你長相守。

11 **Will your grandparents come along with your parents to our wedding?**
你的祖父母和你的父母會一起出席我們的婚禮嗎？

Unit 6

Pregnancy & Childbirth

——懷孕生子——

和每個人都聊得來 Track 026

加粗底線字：詳見「超萬用單字／句型」

A: Where is Jason? I haven't seen him at school for a while.	傑森人呢？我有一陣子沒在學校看到他了。
B: Um…It's a long story…you wouldn't want to know this soap drama…	呃……這就說來話長了……你不會想知道這種八點檔的發展的……
A: Hey! What you've said made me even more curious!	欸！你這樣講我反而更好奇了啊！
B: Well, let's make it short. You know the thing between Carol and Jason?	好吧，簡單說，你知道卡蘿和傑森在一起的事吧？
A: Yep! I did hear something. But isn't that a rumor?	對，我是有聽說，可是不是只是傳言而已嗎？
B: It's never been just a rumor, I mean it!	一直都不只是傳言，我說真的！
A: Oh…Goodness! What's wrong with Jason? Dating a nerd like Carol?	喔，天啊！傑森是怎樣？怎麼會跟卡蘿這個書呆子在一起？
B: Calm down…And the worst is that, **Carol's "in trouble" now.**	冷靜點！更慘的是，卡蘿還「有點麻煩」了。

A: No! What the hell is that? Jason and Carol's sweet home?	不會吧！這是怎樣？傑森跟卡蘿要共組甜蜜的家庭了嗎？
B: I'm as shocked as you, cuz Carol **has a baby on the way**, and Jason himself told me about this excitedly.	我跟你一樣驚訝啊，卡蘿都要生了，傑森自己親口很興奮地跟我講的。

超萬用單字／句型

▸ have/has a baby on the way

在歐美國家，懷孕一般不直接説，而是採用比較委婉的表達方式，此句型就表示已成胎而尚未出生的孩子，指婦女懷孕，意為「……快要生孩子了」。

❶ **A: Your mother has a baby on the way, which means you will have a sister or brother.**
→ 你媽媽快要生孩子了，這意味著你快要有一個妹妹或弟弟了。
B: I can't wait to be a big brother! → 哦，我等不及要當哥哥了。

❷ **A: My wife has a baby on the way. Do you know where the nearest hospital is?** → 我妻子快要生了，你知道最近的醫院在哪嗎？
B: Go down this street and then turn right. You will see it.
→ 順著這條路一直走然後右轉，你就會看見了。

▸ she is "in trouble".

一般指未婚女性在不希望的情況下懷孕（比方説：未婚懷孕），意為「她有了麻煩。」此外，其他表達懷孕的方式還有「She is expecting. 她在待產中。」

❶ **A: It has been a long time since I've seen Mary.**
→ 我有很長時間沒看到瑪麗了。
B: I heard that she is in trouble. → 我聽説她有麻煩（未婚懷孕）了。

❷ **A: Do you know that his daughter is in trouble?**
→ 你知道他的女兒未婚懷孕嗎？
B: What? Who's the father? → 什麼？孩子的爸是誰？

實用句型大補帖

1 **She is in a delicate condition.**
她正懷孕中。

2 **She is well-along.**
她懷孕中。

3 **My sister is about to have a blessed event.**
我妹妹將要有喜事（當媽媽）了。

4 **She is about to be in a family way.**
她不久就要走向家庭之路（當媽媽）。

5 **You will be a mother in several months.**
再幾個月之後你就做媽媽了。

6 **The doctor said that she will give birth to a baby in October.**
醫生說她的預產期在十月份。

7 **When do you plan to have a baby?**
你們打算什麼時候懷孕呢？

8 **She is about to have a family.**
她即將要成家了。

9 **Both Lucy and Mary are happy that you successfully delivered a son.**
露西和瑪麗都很高興妳順利產下一個男孩。

10 **When is the expected due date?**
預產期在什麼時候呢？

11 **Which hospital do you want to choose to deliver your baby?**
你準備在哪家醫院生你的孩子呢？

12 **My suggestion is that pregnant woman should be in the hospital in advance .**
我們的建議是孕婦應該提前住院。

13 **Wow, congratulations! The boy takes after his father.**
哇，恭喜你！這孩子長得像他的父親。

Unit 7

Divorce

——離婚——

和每個人都聊得來 Track 027

加粗底線字：詳見「超萬用單字／句型」

A: I think there's a problem going on in our relationship.	我覺得我們之間有點問題。
B: I've told you months ago, but you're just too scared to face it and work out a way with me…	我好幾個月前就告訴你了，但你太害怕以致於不敢面對並和我一起想辦法解決。
A: Well, apparently our passion for love isn't enough to support our married life and all the responsibilities.	嗯，很顯然我們對愛的熱情不足以支撐我們的婚姻生活及所有的責任。
B: You know these are nothing but excuses, right?	你知道這些不過就是藉口，對吧？
A: Whatever you say. **How about** we separate for some time and re-evaluate our relationship?	隨便妳怎麼説吧！不如我們分開一陣子然後重新評估我們的關係吧？
B: **As you know,** I don't want our son to be affected by this…I don't think separation will help.	你也知道，我不希望我們的兒子被這件事影響。我不認為分居有用。
A: Then, what do you suggest?	那妳建議怎麼做？
B: Why don't we go to an expert and seek counseling?	我們為何不尋求專家的諮詢？

A: Do you think those experts can really understand our unsolvable problems?	妳真的認為那些專家能夠瞭解我們難解的問題嗎？
B: Better than never trying. I don't want to be like the Warrens couple. they regretted it right after divorcing each other.	比不努力好吧。我不想像瓦倫斯夫婦一樣，一離婚就後悔了。

超萬用單字／句型

▶ How about...?

外國人在口語對話上常常會用這句話開頭來詢問對方意見或給對方做選擇。如：

❶ **A: I don't know what to eat tonight after class.**
→ 我不知道今晚下課後要吃些什麼。
B: How about we go to the new Thai restaurant?
→ 不然我們去那家新的泰式餐廳如何？

❷ **A: What should we do tonight?** → 我們今晚要幹嘛？
B: How about we invite our friends and have a party?
→ 不然我們邀請我們的朋友來個派對如何？

▶ As you know,...

通常用於陳述對方已經知道或眾所皆知的事情或事實。如：

❶ **A: As you know, Mary has already found a job. What I'm worried about is whether she likes it or not.**
→ 你也知道，瑪莉已經找到工作。我擔心的是她是否喜歡這份工作。
B: Don't worry, I think she loves it. → 別擔心，我想她愛極了。

❷ **A: Why is John eating leaves outside?**
→ 為什麼約翰在外邊吃著樹葉？
B: As you know, he always does strange things.
→ 你也知道，他常做些怪事。

實用句型大補帖

1 **Mandy and Mason decided to separate after 26 years of marriage.**
曼蒂和梅森在結婚26年後決定分居。

2 **Experts say couples should never be afraid to seek counseling if they're struggling.**
專家說婚姻觸礁的夫妻不應害怕尋找婚姻諮詢師。

3 **I want a divorce. I've suffered from our marriage for a long time.**
我要離婚。我已經飽受我們婚姻的摧殘很久了。

4 **They filed for divorce, because they were unable to work out the problems between them.**
他們提出離婚申請，因為他們無法解決他們之間的問題。

5 **My parents have started the divorce proceedings/divorce lawsuit.**
我父母開始打離婚官司。

6 **Let's part on good terms while we can.**
在目前還可以好聚好散的時候分手吧。

7 **It's time to go our separate ways.**
我們分道揚鑣吧。

8 **They split after 10 years of marriage.**
他們結束了10年的婚姻。

9 **Ben announced an amicable split from his wife just one day after their 10 year anniversary.**
班和太太在結婚10週年紀念日隔天宣布和平分手。

10 **I heard that Mary is fighting over her son's guardianship with her husband.**
我聽說瑪莉正在和她丈夫爭奪她兒子的監護權。

11 **Have you heard that Elma divorced her husband earlier this year due to domestic violence issues?**
你知道愛爾瑪年初因為家暴事件與她丈夫離婚嗎？

12 **I heard that she seems to handle the whole divorce really well.**
我聽說她把整個離婚事件處理得很好。

13 **Because of all the unsolvable problems between you and me, I've fallen out of love with you.**
因為一切我們之間無法解決的問題，我已經不再愛你了。

Part 7

聊天哈拉，

絕不錯過和任何人
用英文閒聊的好時機！

Unit 1

Environment

——環保——

和每個人都聊得來 Track 028

加粗底線字：詳見「超萬用單字／句型」

A: Hey! Have you seen Leonardo's new documentary "Before the Flood"?	嘿！你有看過李奧納多那部新紀錄片「洪水來臨前」嗎？
B: No one should miss it! I was so shocked after knowing the truth about "global warming".	絕對不能錯過！當我看完後得知「全球暖化」的真相後超震驚。
A: That's true. I thought this issue was only a popular subject for essays in high school though.	真的。我高中的時候還以為這只是個非常熱門的短文題目呢！
B: Yeah…Only after watching this film did I understand how close we are to "global warming"!	是啊……看完這部我才知道全球暖化和我們有多息息相關。
A: Same. I didn't know even our diet could worsen the "global warming" effect.	我也是啊。我不知道我們連吃的都可以使全球暖化惡化耶。
B: I cried when I saw how human beings burned the rain forests just for their own benefit.	當我看到人們為了自己的利益焚燒雨林時哭了。
A: **Gee!** Did you see those poor orangutans dying from the forest fires set by humans?	哎呀！你也看到那些死於人為森林大火的可憐紅毛猩猩了吧？
B: Yeah…Poor things! No animal **cops** can rescue them from the fire.	有啊……可憐的小東西！沒有動物警察可以拯救牠們……

A: That's a sad story...I think if we don't find a way out, we'll in the end kill ourselves.	真是很悲傷的事……如果我們再不擺脫全球暖化困境，我們最後會害死自己。
B: And all the living things on the Earth will definitely come to an end.	然後使全地球的生物滅絕。

超萬用單字／句型

▶ Gee!

Gee! 意為「唉呀！」，是美國人常用的感嘆詞，表示震驚、惱怒、驚嘆等意思，韓國女團曾以此感嘆詞作為歌曲名。

❶ **A: I forgot to bring my homework.** → 我忘記帶家庭作業了。
B: Gee! Miss Wang will never forgive you, and she will give you a punishment. → 哎呀，王老師不會原諒你的，她會處罰你的。

❷ **A: Gee! How can you leave me here and go back home by yourself?** → 唉呀！你怎麼能把我獨自丟在那自己回家呢？
B: There's been a misunderstanding. I went back home to get a coat for you. → 這是誤會，我只是回家幫你拿外套。

▶ cop

美國人在口語裡很少用 policeman 來表示警察，而用 cop 來形容。報警的電話號碼是 911。有時候，美國人也用 911 來表示緊急的事。另外，美國人提到 911 電話的時候會說 nine-one-one, 而不是 nine-eleven.

❶ **A: If you continue to disturb me, I will call the cops.**
→ 如果你繼續騷擾我的話，我就報警了。
B: Oh, Kate, I just want to talk to you. You know, I love you.
→ 凱特，我只是想和你說說話，你知道，我愛你。

❷ **A: Although the cop came, the thief still ran away.**
→ 儘管最終警察來了，但小偷還是跑了。
B: I guess you should try to solve the problem by yourself.
→ 我猜你得自己想辦法解決這個問題了。

實用句型大補帖

1 **The earth's climate is getting warmer.**
全球氣候變得越來越暖和。

2 **Gee! How could you litter everywhere?**
哎，你怎麼能到處亂丟垃圾呢？

3 **The environmental damage has become a serious threat to humankind.**
環境破壞對人類來說是嚴峻的威脅。

4 **Please remember the World Environment Day. It's on the 5th of June.**
請記住世界環保日：6月5日。

5 **The main threat to penguins today is the loss of their icy habitat due to climate change.**
企鵝最大的威脅是因氣候變遷而逐漸消失的冰寒棲息地。

6 **If we don't protect the environment, all the living things in the world will come to an end one day.**
如果我們不懂得保護環境，總有一天世界上所有的生物都會滅亡。

7 **The factory in the city expels industrial waste day and night.**
城市裡的工廠日夜都在排放工業廢物。

8 **Can we call the cops when someone kills a dolphin?**
當有人獵殺海豚時，我們能報警嗎？

9 **The global warming will lead to the extinction of some animals.**
全球暖化會導致某些動物滅絕。

10 **Hope all the people in the world can protect the environment and animals.**
希望全世界的人都能保護環境和動物。

Unit 2

Technology

——科技——

和每個人都聊得來 Track 029

加粗底線字：詳見「超萬用單字／句型」

A: Did you see Sharp's newly released phone Robot, RoBoHoN?	你有看到夏普最近推出的新手機機器人，RoBoHoN嗎？
B: I saw the advertisement! Oh my God! The little robot is so cute!!	我看到廣告了！天啊！這個小機器人真是太可愛了啦！
A: Yep! It's tiny and delicate! You can even have a conversation with it!	對啊！又小又精緻！！你還可以跟它對話喔！
B: **This rocks!** It has every function that a smartphone has.	這太酷了！它甚至具備所有智慧型手機的功能。
A: That's the most amazing part! But what exactly is it, a phone or a robot?	這就是它酷的地方！但是它到底是手機還是機器人啊？
B: Let's search related articles about RoBoHoN on Google!	我們在辜狗搜索一下RoBoHoN相關文章吧！
A: Great idea! Look! This article calls RoBoHoN robotic pal…	好主意！看！這篇文章稱呼RoBoHoN為機器人朋友……
B: It also says that RoBoHoN is controlled all by human voice!	它也說RoBoHoN是完全以人聲操控的！
A: That's really cool! I really want this robotic pal to stay with me all the time…	真的太酷了！我好想要一個機器人朋友一直陪著我……

B: Um...If you **brown nose** me, perhaps I can buy you one!

嗯……如果妳討好我，搞不好我可以買一台送妳！

超萬用單字／句型

This rocks!

Rock 在英語口語俚語中表示「很棒、時髦和很帥」，是當今英美等國家年輕人比較常見的表達方式，在意義上同「cool」一致。常用於讚美別人。

❶ **A: I have already passed the exam, Tom.**
→ 湯姆，我已經通過考試了。
B: You rock! Why not hold a party?
→ 你真是太帥了，為什麼不辦個派對呢？

❷ **A: This song rocks. It's been dominating the charts for weeks.**
→ 這首歌很厲害，已經佔據排行榜第一名好幾個禮拜了。
B: I've got to have a listen then. → 那我得來聽聽看。

brown nose

brown-nose（拍馬屁）是因為奉承地親別人的屁股使得鼻頭沾上對方的糞便，才會產生咖啡色鼻頭。「brown-nose」這個字就是因為上述的意象而用來表示拍馬屁、奉承的意思，名詞是指拍馬屁這種行為，而名詞 brown-noser，則表示拍馬屁的人。

❶ **A: Mom, can you buy a computer for me? I want one very much.** → 媽媽，能買台電腦給我嗎？我非常想要一台。
B: No, but I can consider it if you brown nose me.
→ 不，不過你要是能巴結我，倒是可以考慮一下。

❷ **A: Why don't you like her?** → 你為什麼不喜歡她呢？
B: She is a famous brown-noser in our class.
→ 她是我們班出名的馬屁精。

實用句型大補帖

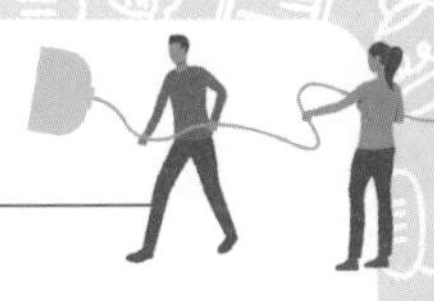

1 **Do you know what robotics is?**
你知道什麼是機器人學嗎？

2 **Robotics is the branch of mechanical engineering, electrical engineering and computer science that deals with the design, construction, operation, and application of robots.**
機器人學是一項涵蓋了機器人的設計、建造、運作、以及應用的跨領域科技。

3 **This rocks! Does that mean you have really seen a UFO?**
這太帥了，意思是說你真的看到過UFO囉？

4 **You can brown-nose me if you want me to buy you an iPhone.**
如果你想要我買一台iPhone給你的話，那就巴結巴結我吧！

5 **The scientist said that one day all the housework can be done by a robot.**
科學家說未來某天所有的家事都可以由機器人來完成。

6 **So far , I have never seen aliens like what other people talked about.**
到目前為止，我還沒有看到人們所說的外星人。

7 **What does NASA stand for?**
NASA這個單字代表的是什麼意思呢？

8 **You must keep all the details under control in order to complete the spacecraft landing.**
為了能讓太空船順利登陸，你必須保證每個細節都在掌握中。

9 **Developments in technology give us greater convenience.**
科技的發展給我們帶來了更好的便捷。

10 **It has been more than fifty years since Gagarin was sent to the outer space.**
距離加加林被送往太空已經超過五十年了。

Unit 3

Education

——教育——

和每個人都聊得來 Track 030

加粗底線字：詳見「超萬用單字／句型」

A: Why do you look so exhausted? What's wrong?	你為什麼看起來那麼累？怎麼了？
B: Nothing much...Just that our finals will start next week.	沒什麼啦……就下禮拜開始期末考了。
A: Oh...So you pulled an all-nighter studying for the whole week?	噢……所以你一整個禮拜熬夜唸書嗎？
B: **Duh**, I failed almost every quiz in most of my classes...you know that!	還用說嗎？我每堂課的小考幾乎都不及格……你也知道啊！
A: **What's your** average **score** for the quizzes?	你小考平均都幾分啊？
B: It's between 58 and 59.5. I don't know why it's always under 60...	大概都在58分到59.5之間吧。我不知道為什麼總是低於60……
A: Well...It's not all your fault, I think your teachers also need to take some responsibility for that.	嗯……也不全都是你的錯，我覺得你的老師們多少也得負點責任。
B: I don't want to blame them and myself...after all the effort...	我不想責備他們或我自己……在都盡了一切努力後……

A: Hey! Cheer up! Maybe you are just not used to the education system here…	嘿！打起精神！或許你只是不習慣這裡的教育體制而已……
B: Yeah… maybe I have studied abroad for too long…	是啊……或許我在國外讀書太久了……

超萬用單字／句型

▶ What's your score...

此句型多用於問對方課業成績或者是考試分數，是同學、老師及家長彼此之間非常直接的詢問方式，意為「……得了多少分？」，相同意義的表達方式還有「How was your score? 你的成績怎麼樣？」

❶ **A: Mary, what is your score in the math examination?**
→ 瑪麗，你的數學考了幾分？
B: Oh, it's a secret. → 嗯，是個秘密。

❷ **A: How was your score in Chinese?**
→ 你中文考試的成績怎麼樣？
B: I don't know. The professor said that I will have a high score. → 我不知道，教授說我還滿高分的。

▶ Duh

Duh 是美國人用來表示「這還用說嗎？」等所發出來的一種語音。說的時候要有一種有點像說中文的「廢話！」那樣的語氣。

❶ **A: I heard that you want to live with him?**
→ 我聽說你要和他同居了？
B: Duh, do I have another choice?
→ 還用說嗎？我還有別的選擇嗎？

❷ **A: Do you really love me?** → 你真的愛我嗎？
B: Duh, you are everything to me. I really don't want to lose you. → 還用說嗎？你是我的一切，我真的不想失去你。

實用句型大補帖

1 **What score did you get in this exam?**
你這次考試得了多少分？

2 **The education in our country will make us second to none in scores.**
我們國家的教育體制就是讓我們在考試上名列前茅。

3 **How was your score in math?**
你數學成績怎麼樣？

4 **Nowadays, more and more parents let their children go abroad to have a better education.**
現在，越來越多的父母讓他們的孩子出國去接受更好的教育。

5 **What is your best subject?**
你成績最好的是哪一科？

6 **Duh, the schooling system in England is not as same as in Taiwan.**
還用說嗎？英國的學制和台灣的當然不一樣了。

7 **There are two kinds of courses for you to choose, the optional courses and the compulsory courses.**
有兩種課程可供你選擇，選修課和必修課。

8 **I would like to go to the library to read books by Freud.**
我想到圖書館去看佛洛伊德的書。

9 **Don't overdo it. Get some rest if you feel tired.**
不要過度用功，如果累的話就休息一下子。

10 **The teacher will give us a quiz every week.**
每週老師都會給我們小考。

11 **Frankly speaking, if you really want to learn some useful knowledge, you should go and study at the Sorbonne.**
坦白說，如果你真要學習實用的知識，你應該到索邦大學學習。

Unit 4

Film & TV

——影視——

和每個人都聊得來 Track 031

加粗底線字：詳見「超萬用單字／句型」

A: My colleagues strongly recommended me to see the Korean movie "Train to Busan" in the cinema.	我同事們強力推薦我去電影院看「屍速列車」。
B: Oh! That popular movie! People around me are all discussing this movie. It looks like a zombie movie at first glance though...	噢！那部很紅的電影！我身邊的人全部都在討論它。第一眼看起來像喪屍片⋯⋯
A: **How disgusting!** I hate zombies! Are you sure this is a nice movie?	好噁喔！我討厭喪屍！你確定這是部好片嗎？
B: But most of the positive comments says that it's more than a **lame** horror movie.	但超多正面評論說它不只是一部差勁的恐怖片。
A: Yeah, my colleagues said it reflects human instincts, and you can see the best part of humans and the worst.	是喔，我同事們也說這部片反應人性，你可以在片中看到人性最光輝和最黑暗的一面。
B: Sounds quite interesting! How about going to cinema and watching it now?	聽起來很有趣耶！要不要現在直接去電影院看？
(At the cinema...)	（在電影院⋯⋯）
B: Please give me 2 adult tickets in the front area.	請給我兩張前排的成人票。
A: Sorry, there're no tickets left for the front row. Is the middle area also ok?	不好意思，前排座位的票已經售完了。中間的位置可以嗎？

(After the movie...)	（電影結束後……）
A: I cried. I was deeply touched. All the actors put on a good performance.	我被這部電影深深的打動了，所有的演員都演得很精彩。
B: I agree. Even the actors who played those zombies put on a good performance!	我也有同感。連那些演喪屍的演員都演得很棒！

超萬用單字／句型

▶lame

lame 在這是「很差勁」的意思，此外 lame 還有「跛腳的、不高明的」意思。相同意義的單字還有「sucks」。

❶ **A: The people here are so lame; I can't stand them.**
→ 這裡的人太差勁了，我簡直無法忍受。

B: You should try to get to know them better.
→ 你應該嘗試多認識他們。

❷ **A: Do you like to watch any TV programs? Like talk shows?**
→ 你喜歡看電視節目嗎？類似於脫口秀？

B: No, I think those are lame. → 不，我覺得那種的很差勁。

▶How disgusting!

How disgusting 常用於表示極度厭惡、討厭及反感的情緒，意為「噁心、討厭、無聊」等。是歐美人士表達極度的情感體驗的常用詞。

❶ **A: I heard that she fell in love with her brother.**
→ 我聽說她和她的哥哥相愛了。

B: How disgusting! It's forbidden love!
→ 多噁心啊！這是禁忌的愛。

❷ **A: How disgusting. You only wash your hair once a week.**
→ 你一星期只洗一次頭，多噁心哪！

B: It's very normal in cold countries.
→ 在很冷的國家是很正常的。

實用句型大補帖

1 **That movie was so lame. I didn't even stay through the whole film.**
那部電影實在太爛了，我甚至沒看完。

2 **I heard that there's an interesting film showing this weekend.**
我聽說週末有一部很吸引人的電影上映。

3 **Please use the remote control to turn down the volume. I want to sleep.**
請用遙控器把音量調小，我想睡覺了。

4 **There's a football match on channel 5. Would you please switch it on for me?**
第五台有一場足球賽，你能幫我轉台嗎？

5 **I'm sure you will like today's program.**
我確定你會喜歡今天的節目。

6 **What price is the ticket, please?**
請問票價多少錢？

7 **Please give me one adult and one child ticket.**
請給我一張成人票和一張兒童票。

8 **What do you think of the main actor of this film?**
你怎麼評價這部電影的男主角？

9 **Sorry, there're no tickets left for the front row.**
不好意思，前排座位的票已經售完了。

10 **How disgusting! I really hate watching horror movies.**
多噁心啊！我真的很討厭看恐怖片。

11 **I'm deeply moved by the film. All the actors put on a good performance.**
我被這部電影深深的打動了，所有的演員都演得很精彩。

12 **Not everyone likes to go to the cinema to watch movies.**
不是所有人都喜歡到電影院去看電影。

Unit 5

Media

——傳媒——

和每個人都聊得來 Track 032

加粗底線字：詳見「超萬用單字／句型」

A: Oh...Today's CNN news makes me want to **catch some Zs**... (yawning)	噢……今天的CNN新聞讓我想睡……（打哈欠）
B: No way! They reported so much about the election campaign.	不會吧！他們今天報超多大選活動耶！
A: Come on... watch that clown play tricks and say some stupid things?	拜託……看那個小丑玩把戲和說蠢話嗎？
B: Don't you think he's the most interesting part of the election? Otherwise it could be so boring.	妳不覺得這是大選最有趣的部分嗎？要不然會很無聊耶。
A: Do you like that crazy, childish guy? So, you're gonna vote for him?	你喜歡那個瘋狂、幼稚的傢伙？所以你要投他？
B: **Got you!** I just want to have some fun in regular daily life, and he's the best clown!	嚇到妳了！我只是想在平凡的日常生活中找點樂子而已，他就是最佳丑角！
A: Yeah...seems that he brought you so much joy, huh?	是啊……他為你帶來很多歡樂對吧？

B: Sure! But I'll never vote for someone who doesn't respect females!	當然！但我絕不會投不尊重女性的候選人！
A: Unless you want to become the enemy of all the women in the nation!	除非你想成為全國女性公敵！

超萬用單字／句型

▶ catch some Zs

記不記得漫畫裡的人睡覺，旁邊都畫「Z,Z,Z...」，所以英文中 catch some Zs 就是這樣來的。「我要小睡一會」就可以這樣説「I have to catch some Zs.」相同意義的表達方式還有「I have to take a nap./ I need to snooze.」。

❶ **A: Oh, I have to catch some Zs. Would you please wake me up when the teacher comes in?**
→ 我要小睡一會，你可以在老師進來的時候叫醒我嗎？
B: OK, if you dare, you can. → 好的，如果你敢睡的話就睡吧。

❷ **A: I always feel sleepy in Mr. Green's class.**
→ 我總是在上格林先生的課時想睡覺。
B: You can catch some Zs during the break.
→ 你可以在休息的時候小睡一會。

▶ Got you!

Got you 意為「（騙、嚇、捉弄……）到你了吧！」，但具體的意思還要放在特定的句子裡來看。此外，它還有「明白了」的意思，I don't get it 就是我不明白的意思。

❶ **A: What? You said that you fell in love with your sister?**
→ 什麼？你説你愛上了你的妹妹？
B: Got you! → 騙到你了吧！

❷ **A: What are you talking about? I don't get it.**
→ 你們在説什麼？我不明白。
B: It's because you are too stupid. → 那是因為你太笨了。

實用句型大補帖

1 **Today's cover story of *World* Magazine:"Are you Racist?"**
本日世界雜誌的封面故事是關於：你有種族歧視嗎？

2 **Compared to the radio, I prefer to watch TV.**
和收音機比起來，我還是喜歡看電視。

3 **My father likes to read the papers every morning.**
我父親喜歡每天早上看報紙。

4 ***The Times* is very hot in demand .**
《時代》雜誌很熱門。

5 **I have to catch some Zs. call me when the delivery man comes.**
我要小睡一會，送貨員來了再叫我。

6 **Newspapers not only tell you the important things that happened in the world, but also broaden your knowledge.**
報紙不僅可以使你瞭解世界各地的重要事情，還可以豐富知識。

7 **I have been a subscriber for three years.**
我已經訂購3年了。

8 **How much does it cost to subscribe?**
訂購要多少錢？

9 **Do you often read newspapers?**
你經常看報紙嗎？

10 **Got you! You should read it once again more carefully.**
上當了吧！你應該再仔細地讀一遍。

11 **I want to cancel the subscription; what about you?**
我想取消訂購，你呢？

12 **The paper is rich in content and succinct in style. We all really like to read it.**
這報紙內容豐富，文字簡潔，我們大家都很喜歡看。

13 **My parents and I get the news either by TV or the newspaper.**
我和我的父母透過電視或者報紙看新聞。

Unit 6

Anecdote

——奇聞——

和每個人都聊得來 Track 033

加粗底線字：詳見「超萬用單字／句型」

A: I have read a book about child marriage, it is called"I Am Nujood, Age 10 and Divorced".	我剛讀完一本有關童婚的書，叫作「我叫諾珠，我10歲離過婚」。
B: Jesus Christ! A 10-year-old girl should be in the classroom of elementary school!	天啊！一個10歲小女孩應該在國小教室裡。
A: Yeah...That's really creepy for us. Guess where she is from?	對啊……對我們來說超詭異。猜猜她是哪國人？
B: India, a country notorious for child marriage.	印度，以童婚聞名的國家。
A: **Bingo!** It's even illegal in India, but they have this kind of custom...	答對啦！童婚在印度甚至是違法的，但是他們有童婚習俗。
B: No wonder...How about little boys in India?	難怪……那印度的小男孩呢？
A: The same...Some even get married at age 4...	一樣……有些甚至4歲就結婚了……
B: Hey! It's just my little boy's age! Are they crazy?	嘿！跟我兒子一樣大！他們瘋了嗎？

A: Exactly! I am glad that your little **lady killer** doesn't have to go through this!	是啊！我很高興妳們家小少女殺手不用經歷這些！
B: I also feel I'm lucky that I was born here!	我也覺得我出生在這裡好幸運！

超萬用單字／句型

▶ lady killer

lady killer 意為「少女殺手」，注意 killer 不僅僅指「殺手」的意思，同時還表示「有吸引力的、迷人的、厲害的」的意思，相當於中文裡的「致命吸引力」。例如：killer app 意為「高級的、先進的應用程式」。

❶ **A: If you keep working out, you will be a lady killer one day.**
→ 如果你持續健身，有一天你將成為少女殺手。
B: Oh, really? I hope that day comes sooner.
→ 真的嗎？那我希望那一天能快點到來。

❷ **A: I will get married, have a cute boy and make him a lady killer.** → 我會結婚生子，有個可愛的男孩然後讓我的兒子成為少女殺手。
B: That way, I will make my child a man killer.
→ 那樣的話，我就讓我的孩子成為少男殺手。

▶ Bingo!

Bingo 是一種填寫格子的遊戲，在遊戲中第一個成功者以喊「Bingo」表示取勝而得名。現今在英語中意為「猜對了、正確」。此外，它還指因出乎意料的成功而興奮的叫聲。

❶ **A: Is this your pencil?** → 這是你的鉛筆嗎？
B: Bingo! I finally found it. Thank you so much!
→ 哇！我終於找到它了，謝謝你喔！

❷ **A: You are very nervous, am I right?** → 你很緊張，對嗎？
B: Bingo! You are so clever. → 你猜中了！你真聰明。

實用句型大補帖

1 **In Baltimore, parents can serve up to a year in jail if convicted of allowing their children to skip class.**
在巴爾的摩，縱容孩子翹課的家長將面臨最高一年的監禁。

2 **I heard that an old woman was addicted to eating ants.**
我聽說有一位老婦人對吃螞蟻上癮。

3 **A report revealed yesterday that math teachers in England are among the most poorly trained.**
一份研究報告指出，英國的數學老師最未經過良好訓練。

4 **It is said that he became a lady killer when he was only one year old.**
據說他在一歲的時候就成為少女殺手了。

5 **An American girl called Felicia Frisco dares to sleep with a six month-old Bengal tiger!**
一名叫做菲利希亞．弗里斯克的美國女孩敢與一頭六個月大的孟加拉虎「同床共枕」。

6 **Bingo! You are right, the British love dogs more than humans.**
你猜對了，英國人喜歡狗勝於人。

7 **The report said that an elderly Spanish farmer used waste materials to build an extraordinary cathedral.**
報導指稱一位西班牙老農用垃圾建造了一座宏偉的教堂。

8 **In order to enlarge the vocabulary of students, the teachers in England had their students copy the dictionary.**
為了增加學生的辭彙量，英國的老師竟然讓學生們抄字典。

9 **You are as clever as a computer.**
你像電腦一樣聰明。

10 **A new poll has revealed that wearing glasses ages people by at least three years.**
一項最新調查顯示，戴眼鏡會讓人看起來至少老3歲。

Unit 7

Gossip

——八卦——

和每個人都聊得來 Track 034

加粗底線字：詳見「超萬用單字／句型」

A: You know what? My friend's uncle was Julian Merltz's high school classmate.	妳知道嗎？我朋友的叔叔是朱利安・梅爾茲的高中同學。
B: Really? You mean that candidate of the D Party?	真的是這樣？你說那個D黨候選人？
A: Bingo!	答對了！
B: Is it another April fool's joke? It's April first.	這是另一個愚人節玩笑嗎？今天是4月1日。
A: No, I mean what I said.	不，我說真的。
B: What was he like when he was young?	他年輕時怎麼樣啊？
A: I don't care much about his high school gossip. Instead, I'm more worried about if he can take the lead in popularity polls.	我不是很在意他高中的八卦。我反而比較關心他的民調是否可以領先。
B: Well, according to the newly released poll, his rival has gradually **turned the tables**.	嗯，根據最新民調顯示，他的對手已經慢慢領先了。
A: Do you know about his scandals? And he's quite naive as a politician…	妳知道他的醜聞嗎？還有他是一個蠻幼稚的政治人物。

B: For me, a gentleman like Julian who **is wearing two hats** may not be healthy enough to take responsibility for being a governer.

對我來說，像朱利安這樣忙碌的人的健康或許不足以使他肩負州長的大任。

超萬用單字／句型

▶ turned the tables

turn the table 字面意思是「掀翻桌子」，很容易讓人誤解為是生氣的意思，其實恰恰相反，在英語國家，這一用法意為「轉敗為勝、轉弱為強」，表示局勢的扭轉。

❶ **A: They said that we should lower the quoted price. What should we do?** → 他們要求我們降低報價，我們該怎麼辦呢？

B: Don't worry about that. I can turn the tables in the negotiation. → 不要擔心，我會在談判中扭轉局勢的。

❷ **A: Do you think that Japan can turn the tables in the economic crisis?** → 你認為日本能在經濟危機中扭轉局勢嗎？

B: I don't think so, because it's a worldwide crisis.
→ 我不認為，因為這畢竟是全球性的危機。

▶ Sb be wearing two hats.

wear two hats 並不是字面上戴兩頂帽子的意思，歐美國家通常用這表示某人很忙或身兼多職，所以英文中有些詞語是有詞外之意的，注意不要鬧出笑話。

❶ **A: She is wearing two hats. It's too hard to see her.**
→ 她可是大忙人，見到她太不容易了。

B: I know. She is a workaholic. → 我知道！她真是個工作狂。

❷ **A: My life is so empty. I hope I can get to wear two hats one day.** → 我的人生太空虛了，我希望某天能忙起來。

B: You can go get a part time job. → 你可以兼職阿。

實用句型大補帖

1. **Would you please tell me some things about Bill Gates?**
你能告訴我一些關於比爾蓋茲的事嗎？

2. **I heard from David that he knows him very well.**
我聽大衛說他跟他很熟。

3. **His agent turned the tables after the scandal was reported by the media.**
他的醜聞被媒體揭露後，經紀人幫他扭轉局面。

4. **You know what? The famous singer Britney was once a friend of mine.**
你知道嗎，著名歌星布蘭妮曾經是我的朋友。

5. **As a loyal fan of Johnny Depp, I really want to know more about his private life.**
作為強尼戴普的忠實粉絲，我真的很想知道更多他的私生活。

6. **They are wearing two hats, so they have no time to hold a concert.**
他們實在是太忙了，沒有時間舉辦演唱會。

7. **Nowadays, the movie stars are treated as people from the upper society.**
現在，電影明星被認為是上流社會的人。

8. **It is said that a woman committed suicide because he got married.**
據說有個女人因為他結婚而自殺了。

9. **It is his sexual relationship with another woman that caught the media's attention.**
他與另外一位女人的性關係引起媒體的注意。

10. **I want to know everything about Madonna. The more, the better.**
我想知道關於瑪丹娜的所有事情，越多越好。

11. **I'm very interested about how celebrities deal with their scandals.**
我對於名人們如何處理他們的醜聞很感興趣。

12. **Are you kidding? She is a very famous person in this area.**
你在開玩笑嗎？她可是這個領域大名鼎鼎的人物。

13. **After the outbreak of the scandal, she has tried so many times to kill herself.**
在醜聞爆發之後，她多次企圖自殺。

Unit 8

Pressure

——壓力——

和每個人都聊得來 Track 035

加粗底線字：詳見「超萬用單字／句型」

A: Hey! Melina, your face looks really pale! Are you alright?	嘿！瑪琳娜，妳的臉色好蒼白喔！妳還好嗎？
B: Not really...I have worked overtime and stayed up for 3 days...	不是很好……我已經超時工作又熬夜3天了……
A: My God! Why?	天啊！為什麼？
B: I have been **under** great **pressure** these days. Remember that group project?	我最近壓力超大。記得那個小組專案嗎？
A: Of course. But isn't that the responsibility of the group leader?	當然。但那不是組長的責任嗎？
B: It should be...but our leader is on maternity leave, and I was appointed to take over this...	原本是。但是我們組長請產假，然後我被任命負責這個項目。
A: So it's only Jason and you now?	所以現在都是妳和傑森在做嗎？
B: Now you know that...	妳現在知道了吧……

A: Oh…Look at the bright side, at least you have Jason.	噢……往好處想，至少妳還有傑森。
B: Not anymore, he has taken a sick leave for 3 days because of **diarrhea**.	沒有了，他已經因為腹瀉請了3天病假。

超萬用單字／句型

▸ under pressure

通常用於工作場所，尤其多用於面試官詢問應聘者，藉以考察應聘者是否能在高強度壓力下工作，並且勝任此項工作。

❶ **A: Can you work under great pressure?**
→ 你能在高強度的壓力下工作嗎？
B: Of course, no problem. → 當然，沒問題。

❷ **A: I really want to know how you can work well under the pressure.** → 我很想知道你是如何在壓力下工作？
B: I think the pressure can motivate me to work harder.
→ 我認為壓力可以驅使我更努力工作。

▸ diarrhea

diarrhea 指因水土不服而引起的吃壞肚子、拉肚子症狀。

❶ **A: Why are you so late? Mr. Green is very angry.**
→ 你為什麼遲到了這麼久？格林先生很生氣。
B: I'm sorry, I had diarrhea. → 很抱歉，我拉肚子。

❷ **A: Why do you look so weak?** → 你怎麼看起來那麼虛弱？
B: I have had diarrhea for a week. → 我腹瀉了一個星期。

實用句型大補帖

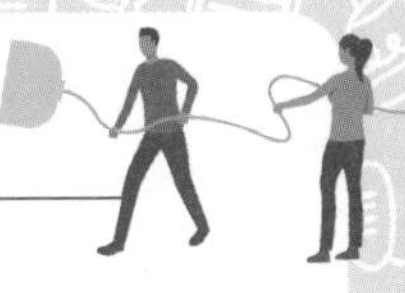

1 **I want to get another job. What's your opinion?**
我想換份工作，你的意見呢？

2 **Can you work well under pressure?**
你能在壓力下將工作做好嗎？

3 **I am really very tired, because I always work overtime.**
我真的太累了，因為我總是超時工作。

4 **He lacks appetite because of the excessive and inflexible working hours.**
過長又沒有彈性的工作時間使他沒有食欲。

5 **At present, I feel I lack passion and control over work.**
現在，我覺得我缺乏對工作的熱情和掌控度。

6 **Could you give me some advice on how to find a new job?**
你能給我一些找新工作的建議嗎？

7 **I can't stand this kind of work. I have no time for love.**
我無法忍受這份工作了，我根本沒有時間談戀愛。

8 **I'm tired of always being under your charge, so I've decided to resign.**
我無法忍受總受你掌控，所以我決定辭職。

9 **He suffers from diarrhea because he is under too much pressure.**
他因工作壓力太大而受腹瀉之苦。

10 **How do you deal with the relationship with your colleagues?**
你是怎麼處理和同事之間的關係？

11 **Although the work is boring, I will continue to work hard.**
儘管工作很無聊，我還是會努力工作的。

12 **I can work under pressure because I want to challenge myself.**
我能在壓力下工作，因為我想挑戰自己。

Unit 9

Hobbies

—興趣—

和每個人都聊得來 Track 036

加粗底線字：詳見「超萬用單字／句型」

A: How can James just sit in front of the computer for hours?	詹姆斯怎麼可以在電腦前坐好幾個小時啊？
B: Maybe he **has a fascination with** compurters, or…	或許因為電腦很吸引他，或者……
A: Or what?	或者什麼？
B: He was cursed by a computer witch and…	他被電腦女巫詛咒了，然後……
A: Oh…Come on…You think I'll buy that?	噢……拜託……你以為我會相信？
B: Hey, relax…just kidding. Why don't you watch TV first and wait for him?	嘿，放輕鬆……只是鬧一下嘛。妳為什麼不先看電視一邊等他？
A: Watching TV is the most boring thing I could ever think of.	看電視是我可以想到最無聊的事了。
B: Hey, but that's my favorite hobby! **How do you spend your leisure time** if you don't watch TV?	嘿，但那是我第一名的嗜好耶！如果妳不看電視，妳休閒時間都在做什麼？
A: I read and play Klondike Solitaire on the computer!	我閱讀和玩電腦遊戲接龍啊！

B: So, you're here waiting to use the computer just for playing Klondike Solitaire?	所以妳在這裡只是為了等著玩電腦接龍？

超萬用單字／句型

▶ sb. have/has a fascination with

在英文要表達比喜歡更強烈時會用「主詞 + have/has fascination with sth.」，翻譯為「對～著迷」。

❶ **A: Why did you spend so much time staring at those old castles?** → 妳為什麼花那麼多時間看那些舊城堡？

B: I have a certain fascination with old castles.
→ 舊城堡對我具有某種奇特的魅力。

❷ **A: She has been sitting there for hours.**
→ 她已經在裡坐好幾個小時了。

B: She seems to have a fascination with this topic.
→ 這個題目似乎對她很有吸引力。

▶ How do you spend your leisure time?

西方人相當重視興趣愛好的培養，很多父母在孩子很小的時候就有意識培養孩子的業餘愛好等，因此在國外聊彼此的興趣愛好是很好的話題。此句意為「你如何度過你的休閒時光？」，相同的表達方式還有「what's your hobby?/ what do you do in your free time?」。

❶ **A: How do you spend your leisure time, Mary?**
→ 瑪麗，你是如何度過你的休閒時光？

B: I just watch movies, play games and dine with friends.
→ 我只是看看電影、玩遊戲還有和朋友們共進晚餐。

❷ **A: Peter, what do you do in your free time?**
→ 彼得，你空閒的時候都在做些什麼呢？

B: I like to attend parties with my friends.
→ 我喜歡和我的朋友們參加派對。

實用句型大補帖

1 **Do you have any special interests other than watching movies?**
除了看電影外你還有什麼興趣愛好嗎？

2 **What would you like to do in your free time?**
你有空的時候都喜歡做什麼？

3 **Computer games are really very interesting.**
電腦遊戲真的很有趣。

4 **My favorite thing is to eat up all the dishes my mother cooks.**
我最喜歡的事就是吃光媽媽做的每道菜。

5 **How do you entertain yourself after work?**
你下班後怎麼消遣時間？

6 **There's a class that aims at helping people learn English.Would you like to go with me?**
有一個旨在幫助人們學習英語的課程，你要和我一起去嗎？

7 **I find reading novels to be the most interesting thing in my life.**
我覺得閱讀小說是我生活中最有趣的事情。

8 **What about you? Do you like to play basketball, too?**
那你呢？你也喜歡打籃球嗎？

9 **How do you spend your leisure time?**
你是如何度過你的休閒時光？

10 **Are you interested in traveling?**
你對旅遊感興趣嗎？

11 **He considers driving a hobby.**
他把開車視為一種消遣。

12 **It looks as if you are interested in tennis, right?**
你好像對網球很感興趣，對嗎？

Unit 10

Competitions

——競賽——

和每個人都聊得來 Track 037

加粗底線字：詳見「超萬用單字／句型」

A: Did you watch that football **match** between our school and Kinston High School?	你去看了我們學校對金士頓高中的（美式）足球賽嗎？
B: Duh, who didn't?	還用問？誰會沒看？
A: Don't you think it's so breathtaking that the audience area was so quiet?	你不覺得這場超驚險，整場觀眾席都超安靜的嗎？
B: Yeah, our school and Kinston was **neck to neck** until the last quarter.	是啊，我們和金士頓到最後一節以前都勢均力敵。
A: That was really stifling. I held my breath all the time.	那真的很悶。我一直屏息以待。
B: Me, too. My eyes were on our players all the time, afraid of missing any touchdowns.	我也是。我的眼睛一直狂盯我們的隊員，害怕漏掉任何一次達陣。
A: Same for me as well! I was just staring at Menson and Jerry, and praying.	我也是這樣！我一直看著曼森和傑瑞然後祈禱。
B: I really couldn't bear to see Kinston take the lead; I think if they had I would yell really loudly.	我實在沒辦法忍受看到金士頓領先；我想如果他們領先我會狂吼。

A: I am glad that at the last quarter, Menson finally made a touchdown!	我真的很慶幸到最後一節，曼森終於達陣！
B: Thanks to him, we won the champion! He's the hero of our school!	還好有他，我們贏得冠軍！他是我們學校的英雄！

超萬用單字／句型

▶Match

不同的體育比賽在英語中有不同的表達方式，如：match, game, competition,race 等。其中，match 特指對手之間比勝負的比賽，競賽等，如，basketball match 籃球比賽，同時也可指體育項目外的各種比賽。

❶ **A: Would you like to watch the tennis match tomorrow afternoon with me?** → 你願意明天下午和我一起去觀看網球比賽嗎？
B: Of course I'd like to since I have nothing to do.
→ 當然願意，反正我也沒事做。

❷ **A: I often watch the campus football matches during the years in school.** → 在學校那段歲月我經常觀看校園足球賽。
B: Me too. → 我也是。

▶neck and neck

這個片語來自賽馬，原本是指兩匹馬跑得並駕齊驅，「肩並肩、脖子並脖子」。後來，這個片語也就衍生為「兩方不相上下的樣子」。

❶ **A: What's going on now?** → 現在局勢如何？
B: Daphne and Mary are neck and neck in the competition.
→ 黛芙妮和瑪莉在比賽中的表現不分上下。

❷ **A: The two players were neck to neck ever since the beginning stage.** → 兩位選手在比賽一開始就並駕齊驅。
B: Naturally, they became joint champions in the end.
→ 很自然地，最後兩人並列第一。

實用句型大補帖

1 **I hope I won't miss the football match.**
我希望我不會錯過足球賽。

2 **How many laps can you swim?**
你能來回游幾趟？

3 **The Spanish runner finally carried off the gold medal in the match.**
在這場比賽中西班牙跑者最終奪得金牌。

4 **It was her first international sports event.**
這是她第一次的國際體育比賽。

5 **Do you know who the gold medalist in this match is?**
你知道這次比賽的金牌獲獎者是誰嗎？

6 **You should learn some basic techniques if this is the first time you've swum.**
如果這是你第一次游泳的話，你應該學一些基本的技巧。

7 **China is the host country of the 2008 Olympic Games.**
中國是2008年奧運的主辦國。

8 **How do you put so much power into hitting the ball?**
你怎麼能打球打得這麼用力？

9 **I will attend the cheer-section and cry out my love for my team.**
我要加入啦啦隊喊出我對球隊的愛。

10 **As a sportsman, I will never give in to any competition.**
身為一名運動員，我永遠不會向比賽屈服。

11 **He prefers to play tennis rather than play billiards.**
與撞球相比，他更喜歡打網球。

12 **The ball is too high for me to hit an overhead return.**
球太高了，以至於無法將球打回去。

Unit 11

Customs

——風俗——

和每個人都聊得來 Track 038

加粗底線字：詳見「超萬用單字／句型」

A: It's Halloween. Has Janet invited you to her Halloween party?	萬聖節到了耶，珍妮特有邀請妳去她辦的萬聖節派對嗎？
B: Duh, she has invited almost all the students of the school.	還用問嗎？她根本幾乎請了全校的學生。
A: But…not me…	但是……沒有我……
B: Oh…come on, the party's not that important. I will stay with you!	噢……拜託，那個派對一點也不重要，我來陪妳吧！
A: You're really my BFF (best friend forever)!	妳真的是我一輩子最好的朋友耶！
B: Of course! I have spent almost every Halloween with you ever since I could talk.	當然啊！我從會講話開始的每個萬聖節都是跟妳過的耶。
A: That's true. If you go to the party, what would you dress up as?	真的。如果妳會去派對，會裝扮成什麼呢？
B: Keltic Goddess Epona, a protector of horses! Do you know that Halloween originated from the deads' festival of ancient Keltic tradition?	凱爾特女神，埃波娜，她是馬匹的守護者喔！妳知道萬聖節最早是源自凱爾特的亡靈節嗎？

A: Cool! Don't mind me, just go to the party. **Wish you a** great time!	好酷喔！別管我了，妳去派對吧。祝妳玩得開心！
B: Are you sure? **May you have a great Halloween, too!**	妳確定嗎？我希望妳有個快樂的萬聖節！

超萬用單字／句型

▶ May you have a great time!

may表示祝福與願望，多用於書面語中；口語中用時顯得比較莊重。本句型有其獨自的結構形式，may不是在主詞後面，而是擺在句子開頭。may的位置因此顯著，祝願的意義也就隨著突出地表現出來。

❶ **A: I come to tell you that I'm going to Paris to visit my mother.**
→ 我來是要告訴你我準備去巴黎看望我的母親。
B: OK, may you return soon. → 好，祝你早日回來。

❷ **A: I asked the manager to give me a promotion yesterday.**
→ 昨天我請求經理為我升職。
B: May you succeed. → 祝你成功。

▶ Wish you a...

Wish you a...，是「I wish you a...」的省略用法，也是很常用於表示節日祝福的固定用法，意為「祝福妳有一個……」。如：Wish you a Merry Christmas!（祝你聖誕快樂！），Wish you a happy New Year!（祝你新年快樂！）等。

❶ **A: I heard that today is your birthday. I wish you a happy birthday!** → 我聽說今天是你的生日，生日快樂。
B: Thank you very much. You are so kind. → 非常感謝，你真好。

❷ **A: Happy Thanksgiving Day!** → 感恩節快樂！
B: Thanks, wish you a happy Thanksgiving Day, too.
→ 謝謝，你也是。

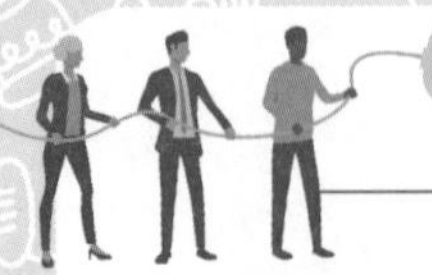

實用句型大補帖

1 **May you have the best New Year!**
願你度過一個最美好的新年！

2 **On Thanksgiving Day, we often eat turkey.**
感恩節的時候，我們通常吃火雞。

3 **I want to dress up as a vampire on Halloween in October.**
我想在十月的萬聖節化妝成吸血鬼。

4 **My father will light up the lights on the Christmas tree on Christmas Eve.**
平安夜，父親會點亮聖誕樹上的燈。

5 **Wish you a Merry Christmas!**
祝你聖誕快樂！

6 **Do you know that Ireland is famous for its ancient Keltic culture?**
你知道愛爾蘭向來以愛爾蘭音樂著稱嗎？

7 **About the origin of Easter Day, it may date back to many years ago.**
關於復活節的起源要追溯到很多很多年前。

8 **Do you know the meaning of Easter Eggs?**
你知道復活節彩蛋的意義嗎？

9 **Finding Easter Eggs is one of the traditional games on Easter Day.**
尋找復活節彩蛋是復活節的傳統遊戲之一。

10 **Wild turkey, garlic and onions and pumpkin pudding are the traditional foods on Thanksgiving Day.**
野生火雞、大蒜和洋蔥及南瓜布丁是感恩節的傳統美食。

11 **Christmas Day in western countries is as important as the New Year in China.**
聖誕節在西方就像新年對中國一樣重要。

12 **I wish I could really see Santa Claus with a big bag of presents with reindeers.**
我希望我能真的看見背著裝滿禮物的大包包的聖誕老人和馴鹿。

Unit 12

Lifestyle

——生活品味——

和每個人都聊得來 Track 039

加粗底線字：詳見「超萬用單字／句型」

A: Work! House work! Responsibility! No, I can't be buried by these!	工作！家務！責任！不，我不能被這些掩埋！
B: Glad you finally figured it out!	很高興妳終於明白了！
A: Yep! I just realized that my life can't just be stuffed with these!	是啊！我終於了解我的人生不能只塞滿這些事！
B: I told you! You have to take care of both your responsibility and your own lifestyle!	早就告訴妳啦！妳要兼顧責任和妳自己的生活品味！
A: Can't agree with you more!	超級同意！
B: So, **may I have the pleasure to** ask my best friend to hang out with me tonight?	所以，我有這個榮幸邀請我的好朋友今晚一起出門嗎？
A: That's my pleasure! Oh, but no one will be there to prepare dinner!	我的榮幸！噢，但是沒人來料理晚餐耶！
B: Spare yourself! You've been focused on others for years! Can't you just think of yourself for a minute?	放過妳自己吧！妳已經為了其他人操心了這麼多年！妳可不可以就花1分鐘為自己著想呢？
A: Sorry…I'm just, just too used to this. I gotta change. **By the bye,** did Marcus take out the garbage…?	抱歉……我只是，只是太習慣這樣了。我一定要改變。對了，馬可斯倒垃圾了嗎？

B: ...A leopard can't change his spots! 牛牽到北京還是牛！

超萬用單字／句型

▶ May I have the pleasure ...?

此句型多用於舞會及大型社交場所或比較正式的場合，多為男士非常紳士的邀請女方跳舞或詢問對方姓名等，是一種非常禮貌的委婉的表達請求的方式。

❶ **A: May I have the pleasure to know your name?**
→ 我能有這個榮幸的知道您的姓名嗎？
B: My name is Linda, L-I-N-D-A.
→ 我叫琳達，L-I-N-D-A。

❷ **A: May I have the pleasure to have dinner with you tonight?**
→ 我今晚能有幸和您共進晚餐嗎？
B: I'm so sorry; I have to go to the hospital to visit my father.
→ 我很抱歉，我得到醫院去看望我的父親。

▶ By the bye,...

意思與「By the way,…」相同。都是語氣詞，一般用於轉移話題或是掩飾即將進行話題的嚴肅性等，一般表示隨意的轉折性，意為「順帶一提……」。

❶ **A: By the bye, could you please tell me why you are so sad?**
→ 順便問一下，能告訴我為什麼你這麼悲傷嗎？
B: I don't know. I just want to see my mother right now.
→ 不知道，我只想馬上見到我媽。

❷ **A: Tom said he will dine with you tonight, did he?**
→ 湯姆說他今晚和你共進晚餐，對不對？
B: Yeah, it's our first date. By the bye, could you recommend me some places for dinner? → 是啊，這是我們的第一次約會。順便問一下，能推薦我一些吃飯的地方嗎？

實用句型大補帖

1 **May I have the pleasure of having this dance with you?**
我能有幸邀請您跳支舞嗎？

2 **Helen likes the tango and she dances well in the dancing party.**
海倫喜歡探戈並且在舞會中跳的很好。

3 **Let's go to the bar and have some fun!**
我們去酒吧找點樂子吧！

4 **I often go to the KTV with my friends after work.**
我下班後通常和朋友們去KTV。

5 **I'd like the cocktail you made for me last time.**
我想喝上次你調給我喝的雞尾酒。

6 **By the bye, would you like to have a cup of coffee with me?**
順便問一下，願意和我喝杯咖啡嗎？

7 **The band at this night club is first rate .**
這間夜店裡的樂團是一流的。

8 **Don't fight against fashion. Go and dye your hair.**
不要和時尚作對，去染一下你的頭髮吧！

9 **She is a party animal and has a lot of friends.**
她是個派對咖，而且擁有很多朋友。

10 **He's hunting for his mate tonight.**
他在找他今晚的女伴。

Part 8

投資理財，

搞懂財經英文口語、在哪裡都能做好財務規劃！

Unit 1

Expenses

——支出——

和每個人都聊得來 Track 040

加粗底線字：詳見「超萬用單字／句型」

A: Ah! I really wanna fly to Guam and have a long, long vacation there!	啊！好想飛到關島渡個超長假喔！
B: That must cost a great deal of money...	那要花超多錢吧……
A: Absolutely! That's why I'm still here... But I really wanna go there sooner!	對啊！所以我還在這裡……但真的好想早點去喔！
B: **It seems** that you have to cut your daily expenses and save more these days.	那你似乎得縮減你的日常開銷然後多存點錢了。
A: Oh...No! Just imagine not being able to go to the Spa Center as often as I do now...	噢……不！想想我不能像現在一樣經常去Spa中心了……
B: How often do you go there then? Twice a week?	妳多久去一次呢？一週兩次嗎？
A: No, I need to go there at least four times a week!	不，我至少每週要去4次！
B: ...How much does it cost if you go there almost every day?	……那幾乎每天去要花多少錢啊？

A: Uh…well, I'm a VIP member who can have a discount of 30% every time I go!	呃……嗯，我是VIP會員，所以每次消費可以打七折！
B: That still costs a lot, I bet! This is **the last thing I'll do!**	我賭那還是要花很多錢！我絕對不做這種事！

超萬用單字／句型

▸ ...the last thing I will do.

歐美人士拒絕做什麼事或不情願做某事，習慣用這種句型：That's the last thing... 表示永遠都不想 / 絕對不會做這件事。歐美女士在拒絕男性的追求常說："You are the last boy I'd ever want to marry!"（世界上我最不想嫁的人就是你！）

❶ **A: This is the last thing I will do. You have to believe me!**
→ 我絕對不會對你做這種事的，你要相信我！
B: I trust you! → 我相信你！

❷ **A: Riding a roller coaster is the last thing I'll do.**
→ 我絕對不去坐雲霄飛車。
B: Come on, it is not that bad. → 拜託，沒那麼糟吧。

▸ It seems...

這句可以翻譯為「似乎……」可用在對於事件的發展表示自身的意見時。切記勿與 seen（see 的過去完成式）混淆。

❶ **A: What do you think about Joe and Nina?**
→ 你怎麼看喬和妮娜兩人之間的發展？
B: It seems like they might find a way to get along with each other.
→ 看起來他們兩人可以找到彼此相處的方式。

❷ **A: It seems like a storm is coming.** → 看起來有暴風雨要來了。
B: Yeah, you are right. → 是啊，你說對了。

實用句型大補帖

1 I already spent too much money this month; I need to start saving some for next month.
我這個月已經花了太多錢了，我下個月開始必須要存一點了。

2 I really want to buy an iPad but it will cost me at least $610 dollars, which is too expensive!
我真的很想買一台iPad，不過那會花我至少610元美金，實在太貴了！

3 Sam always keeps his expenses on record, so he will know how much he spends every month. He always goes over it each month to calculate his expenses.
山姆總是會記帳，所以他知道每個月的開銷。他每個月都會檢視一遍，然後計算自己的支出。

4 Do you know how much it will cost to buy the car? It is about a million dollars which is crazy! I will never have enough money to own that car.
你知道要多少錢才能買那輛車嗎？要一百萬美金真是太誇張了！我永遠都不可能有這麼多錢去買這台車。

5 Girls always spend a lot of money on clothes and cosmetics. It seems like they can never resist doing it.
女生們總是花很多錢在衣服和化妝品上，看來她們永遠無法不這麼做。

6 I am going to travel with my friends to Japan, so I need to save money for that!
我準備和我的朋友去日本旅行，所以我需要存點錢！

7 It costs me only a few dollars to get it in the outlet.
它只花了幾塊錢美金就在暢貨中心買到了。

8 Usually the electricity bill will increase a lot for most families in summers, because it is hard not to turn on the air conditioner to deal with the hot weather.
通常夏天的時候家庭的電費都會增加許多。因為天氣熱得讓你很難不開冷氣。

9 She works very hard to earn money because she is a single mother and needs to raise two children by herself.
她非常辛勤的工作賺錢，因為她是單親媽媽又需要獨力扶養兩個小孩。

Unit 2

Deposit

—儲蓄—

和每個人都聊得來 Track 041

加粗底線字：詳見「超萬用單字／句型」

A: Finally you got your first job! We'**re** really **proud of** you, son!	你終於找到了第一份工作！兒子，我們以你為榮！
B: Thanks, Dad! Why did you suddenly mention this?	謝啦，老爸！為什麼突然提這個？
B: Well, it's a milestone in your life, and it's the same for your mom and I.	嗯，這你人生中的里程碑，同時也是你媽和我人生中的里程碑。
A: Sure it is. I'm really grateful for what you and Mom have done for me, especially for providing my university tuition!	當然是。我真的很感恩你和媽為我做的一切，特別是資助我讀大學。
B: That's the last thing we can do for you. Man! That really cost a lot!	那是我們最後能為你做的了。天啊！那可真花了我們不少錢！
A: I'm really lucky that you and Mom regularly save money, so you're able to support me.	我真的很幸運，因為你和媽定期存錢，所以能資助我。
B: Yeah, son, it's quite unusual. Your mom and I have never received any support from your grandparents ever since college.	對啊，兒子。這是很少有的事，你媽和我從專科開始就沒拿到你祖父母一毛的贊助了。
A: So, from now on, I'm gonna start saving money and continue doing it until my retirement!	所以，現在起我要開始存錢直到我退休！

B: Glad to hear that, son. Spending money is always easy compared to saving money, after all.	很高興聽你這麼說，兒子。畢竟，比起存錢，花錢真是超級容易。
A: True! Like what Mom always says: "**You'll never know** what will happen." Maybe I'll need a lot of money the next second.	真的！就像媽常說的：「你永遠不會知道會發生什麼事。」或許我下一秒就會需要一大筆錢。

超萬用單字／句型

▶You will never know...

這一句片語可以解釋為「你永遠不會知道……」，是一句帶有提醒甚至警告意味的句型。句型中的句子時間設定為只有未來可能會發生的事情。

❶ **A: You need to be careful because you will never know what's going to happen next.**

→ 你必須要小心。因為你永遠不會知道接下來會發生什麼事情。

B: I will, thanks for the reminder. → 我會的，謝謝提醒。

❷ **A: Remember to bring an umbrella with you. You will never know when you are going to need it.**

→ 記得帶把傘。因為你不知道什麼時候你會用到它。

B: Ok, I know. → 好的，我知道了。

▶be proud of...

proud 為驕傲之意，不過這是一句讚美詞。通常解釋為我因某件事情或人物感到驕傲。常用於誇讚他人的成就，替對方感到高興時使用。後方所銜接的為名詞片語。

❶ **A: You made it! I am so proud of you!**

→ 你做到了！我真替你感到驕傲！

B: Thank you so much. → 非常謝謝你的誇獎。

❷ **A: Although our team didn't win, I am still proud of our performance.**

→ 儘管我們的隊伍沒有贏，我依舊對我們的表現感到驕傲。

B: I bet the others will be glad to hear that.

→ 我敢說其他人一定會很欣慰你這麼說。

實用句型大補帖

1. **It is important to start saving money when you are young, because you will never know when you will need it.**
年輕的時候就開始存錢是一件很重要的事情，因為你永遠不知道你什麼時候會需要用到。

2. **I hope that one day I could have my own car, so I decided to save money from now on.**
我希望有一天我可以有一台屬於我自己的車，所以我決定從現在開始存錢。

3. **This Harley is my father's favorite; he bought it through years of saving.**
這台哈雷機車是我爸爸的最愛。他花了多年的積蓄買下來的。

4. **My mother always says that young people need to learn to save money once they have a job.**
我媽媽總是説年輕人開始工作後就要學會存錢。

5. **We are going to buy an apartment. It is very nice and big but it might cost us a lot of money, so I will need to get some money from my savings account.**
我們準備買一間公寓，它很漂亮也很大，不過可能會花掉我們不少錢，所以我需要去從我的儲蓄帳戶裡提點錢。

6. **I am so excited because I finally saved my first one million dollars in my life! You know how hard I have tried to control all my expenses to save all this money during the past few years? I am so proud of myself!**
我好興奮，因為我終於存到我人生中的第一個一百萬美元了！你知道這幾年我有多麼努力控制自己的花費來存這筆錢嗎？我真是替我自己感到驕傲！

7. **I wish I'd saved enough money so I could go travel around the world. There are so many places I want to go to.**
我希望我有足夠的積蓄讓我可以去環遊世界。有好多地方我都很想去呢。

8. **I want to go check how much money I have left in my account.**
我想查查看我的帳戶還有多少餘額。

9. **I want to do some investments, such as buying a house or investing in stocks so as to increase my savings.**
我想做一些投資，像是買房或是投資股票來增加我的存款。

10. **Saving money is not an easy thing to do, because people are usually used to spending money faster compared to saving it.**
存錢並不是一件容易的事情，因為人們總是花錢比存錢還來的迅速。

Unit 3

Loan

——貸款——

和每個人都聊得來 Track 042

加粗底線字：詳見「超萬用單字／句型」

A: Oh! What the heck is this?	噢！這是什麼鬼？
B: What's going on? Why did you cry out that loudly?	怎麼了？為什麼叫這麼大聲？
A: See this! (Pointing to the computer screen…)	看這個！（指著電腦螢幕……）
B: Awarded list of scholarship? Where is your name? I didn't see it!	獎學金獲獎名單？你的名字在哪？我沒看到！
A: That's the reason I cried out so loudly! I failed to get the scholarship!	那就是我叫那麼大聲的原因啊！我獎學金申請沒上！
B: Now you'll have to just count on Student Loans. Don't worry, **it's** quite **common**.	那現在你只能靠助學貸款了。別擔心，這對很多學生是很普遍的事。
A: That's really the worst thing I can imagine…What should I do now?	這真的是我想過最糟的狀況了……我現在該怎麼辦呢？
B: First, get to know every detail about Student Loans and their application processes.	首先，去了解所有有關助學貸款和申請手續的細節。

A: I have the information at hand. And then?	我手邊就有資料。然後呢？
B: Go to the bank to apply for it, and decide **how you would like** to pay it off.	去銀行申請助學貸款，然後決定要怎麼還清貸款。

超萬用單字／句型

▶ How would you like...?

是一句詢問句，為禮貌性的用法。第一種常用的方法為句型後方利用 to 來連接動詞，便可以成為一句善意的問句來詢問對方希望怎麼做。

❶ **A: How would you like to cut your hair?**
→ 你希望剪怎麼樣的髮型？
B: Just a little bit shorter. → 只要修短一點就好了。

❷ **A: How would you like your steak to be cooked?**
→ 你希望你的牛排幾分熟？
B: Medium is fine. → 五分熟就好了。

▶ It is common...

Common 意為普遍的，所以這句是用來形容某些現象大眾化和流行。可以根據句中的主詞來變更其連接詞。如果是以名詞開頭的句型便會以 for 作連結。如果是直接談論行為或現象的普遍性，則可以利用 to 來作連接。

❶ **A: Nowadays, it is common for people to have cell phones.**
→ 如今，人人都有手機是很普遍的一件事。
B: Yeah, even young kids can bring one to school.
→ 是啊，甚至連小孩子都能帶手機去上學。

❷ **A: Today, it is common to use computers to solve everything.**
→ 現今，用電腦來處理事情是很普遍的一件事。
B: You are right. We can't live without computers in today's society. → 你說的對。在現在的社會，我們沒有電腦就活不下去了。

實用句型大補帖

1 **We want to buy a new house, but it is too expensive and we don't have enough money, so we have to borrow money from the bank.**
我們想買一棟新的房子，但是太貴了，而且我們沒有足夠的錢，所以我們必須向銀行貸款。

2 **You know it is not good to always take out loans; you must try to get out of debt as soon as possible.**
你知道經常借貸不是一件好事，你一定要試著盡快還清貸款。

3 **Do you know that many American universities provide college loans for students who need to pay the tuition by themselves? Students can pay off the loans after they graduate and get a job.**
你知道美國很多的大學都有提供就學貸款給那些需要自付學費的學生嗎？學生可以等畢業找到工作後再償還學貸。

4 **He tried his best to get to know all about loans.**
他盡一切努力去了解所有關於貸款的事宜。

5 **We have a variety of plans for loans. It depends on your current conditions, your economic status and how you would like to pay for it.**
我們有許多種貸款的方案。這取決於你目前的狀況、你的經濟情況和你打算如何付清貸款。

6 **Sam is in a really bad situation now. He can't pay off his loans, and he is currently working three jobs.**
山姆現在的情況很吃緊。他沒辦法償還他的貸款，而且他現在同時兼三份差了。

7 **If you can maintain your credit and will be able to pay off the money, sometimes taking out a loan is an alternative way to help you deal with economic issues.**
如果你有辦法維持你的信用而且有力還清的話，有的時候貸款是能幫助你處理經濟問題的另一種方法。

8 **I am thinking about applying for college loans, but I am afraid that it might be risky to do so.**
我在考慮要申請大學學貸，不過我害怕這麼做有風險。

9 **It is very common for people to apply for housing loans in America when they want to purchase a house.**
對美國人而言辦理房貸來購屋是一件很普遍的事情。

Unit 4

Investment

——投資——

和每個人都聊得來 Track 043

加粗底線字：詳見「超萬用單字／句型」

A: I wonder how I can own many houses without debt…	我在想我怎麼樣才可以擁有多房而且零負債……
B: There you go again! You should get rich first so as to buy as many houses as you want.	你又來了！為了要買下愈多房子，你應該先變有錢。
A: **Tell me about it!** But how can I become wealthy with only my salary?	我同意！但是我怎麼只靠我的薪水變有錢？
B: Don't even expect that your little salary can make you a millionaire!	別期待你微薄的薪水可以讓你變富翁！
A: Or, I can just lower my living expenses and save more?	或者，我可以縮減生活開支然後存更多錢？
B: You think such a small amount of money can help? Don't be silly!	你覺得你省下的小錢可以幫得上忙？別傻了！
A: Oh…yeah! There is still inflation and the stagnant pay raise to deal with… It's hopeless!	噢…是啊！還有通貨膨脹和凍漲的薪水……好無望！
B: Don't give up so fast! Try some investments, such as gold, stocks or warrants.	別這麼快放棄！試試投資吧，像黃金、股票和權證。

A: Easier said than done! I know little about those investment vehicles!	說比做簡單！我對那些投資工具所知甚少！
B: Then you must **pay attention to** what I'm gonna tell you…	那你一定要注意聽我接下來告訴你的事……

超萬用單字／句型

▸ Pay attention to this,...

外國人在口語對話上常常會為了強調接下來的資訊或者是請對方注意接下來講的部分而用。用法如：

❶ **A: Late assignments will not be accepted and pay attention to this, failing to submit final reports will lead to failing this course!** → 遲交的作業將不會被接受，然後請注意，未繳交期末報告將導致這堂課被當。

B: I see. → 我了解了。

❷ **A: Pay attention to this, all communication devices are banned in the competition.** → 請注意，比賽期間禁止使用任何通訊器材。

B: I can't even use cell phones? → 我連手機也不能用嗎？

▸ Tell me about it!

外國人在口語對話上很常用此句回答對方，意思有時並不一定如字面是「我想知道更多」，有時候可能只是簡單的「當然，我同意」的意思，如：

❶ **A: Mr. Lu is really the best teacher in our school!**
→ 盧老師真的是學校最棒的老師了！

B: Tell me about it! → 當然！

❷ **A: Selphie is really mean to other girls!**
→ 賽爾菲對待其他女孩真是刻薄！

B: Tell me about it! → 我完全同意！

實用句型大補帖

1 **To become wealthy, Investment is a necessary process.**
投資是變有錢的必要過程。

2 **Banks are always launching various investment vehicles, but the risks must be assessed carefully.**
銀行總是推出各種投資工具，但風險必須小心評估。

3 **I want to invest in gold but do not know when the best timing is.**
我想投資黃金卻不知何時是最佳時機。

4 **My next door neighbor has earned a lot of money in recent years because of investment in stocks for his pension.**
隔壁鄰居這幾年因為投資股票賺了不少退休金。

5 **Did you hear that? Patrick lost everything because of a bad decision in the stock market.**
你聽說了嗎？派翠克因為在股票投資中的錯誤決定而失去了一切。

6 **You really should open an account for time deposit, in case you need money but are fired from your company.**
妳真的應該開定存戶頭，以免妳被公司開除後需要用到錢。

7 **Pay attention to this, Elle. By investing a certain amount of money in time deposit in the beginning of each month, you can control your expenses effortlessly.**
聽好了，艾兒，藉由每個月初投資一定金額到定存裡，妳便能輕鬆控制開銷。

8 **Since you have to regularly put money in, the periodic fund investment will force you to make a plan for your living expenses.**
因為你必須定期投入資金，定期定額基金投資就會強迫你規劃生活開銷。

9 **How did you know I'm fond of making investments? Tell me about it!**
你怎麼知道我對投資感興趣？快跟我說。

Unit 5

Insurance

——保險——

和每個人都聊得來 Track 044

加粗底線字：詳見「超萬用單字／句型」

A: Judy, I would like to take a long trip to Poland, Czech Republic and Germany for 20 days.	茱蒂，我想要參加波蘭、捷克、德國20天之旅。
B: Wow! Count me in!	哇！加我一個！
A: Sure! But do you have 20 days? Don't you have to work?	當然好。但是妳空得出20天嗎？妳不是要工作嗎？
B: I work as an insurance agent, so I can arrange my schedule freely!	我是一個保險經紀人，所以我可以很自由安排我的行程表！
A: I envy you! But it isn't easy to be a successful insurance agent like you, right?	好羨慕妳喔！但要當個像妳一樣成功的保險經紀人不容易，對吧？
B: Ha! Thanks for your compliments! I think for this position, all you need is passion and respect.	哈哈！謝謝你的讚美！我想做這個工作你最需要的就是熱情和尊重。
A: Doesn't sound easy for me at all!	聽起來對我來說很不容易！
B: Not that hard, either. My dear friend, **will you be kind enough to** do me a favor?	也沒那麼難。我親愛的好朋友，可以好心幫我個忙嗎？

A: Why not? What can I do for our successful insurance agent?	為什麼不？我可以為我們成功的保險經紀人做些什麼呢？
B: Well, **check it out!** I think we will need this travel insurance….	嗯，看看這個！我想我們會需要這個旅平險……

超萬用單字／句型

▶ Will you be kind enough to...

外國人在口語對話上常為了請別人幫忙而委婉地這樣說，表示「你能不能好心幫我」，如：

❶ **A: Will you be kind enough to help me with my homework?**
→ 你能不能好心幫助我完成作業？
B: Sure. → 當然。

❷ **A: Will you be kind enough to get me some tissues?**
→ 你能不能好心幫我拿一點面紙？
B: No problem! → 當然沒問題！

▶ Check it out!

外國人在口語對話上會想要引起對方注意才說，表示「你瞧，你看，照過來」的意思，用法如：

❶ **A: Check it out! The dog just gave birth to three babies!**
→ 快看！那隻狗狗剛生下了三個小寶寶！
B: Oh! How cute! → 天啊！多可愛！

❷ **A: Check it out! My new stereo set has a high quality sound system!** → 你瞧！我的新音響組有絕佳的音質系統！
B: Cool! → 超酷的！

實用句型大補帖

1 **Mom, I just had a little car accident at the crossroads. Will you be kind enough to tell me the phone number of our insurance company?**

媽，我剛剛在十字路口處出了一點小車禍。妳可不可以好心告訴我保險公司的電話？

2 **I'm sorry, Mr. Wang, but your insurance package does not cover the health of your teeth. You'll have to pay the fee on your own.**

很抱歉，王先生，你的保險專案並不包括牙齒保健的狀況。你可能必須要自己給付費用。

3 **Hey Stacy, I'm thinking about getting insurance for my new born baby. Do you have any good insurance companies to recommend me?**

嘿，史黛西，我想要幫我的寶寶保險。你有推薦的保險公司嗎？

4 **Check it out! We have a special new insurance project! It basically covers every aspect of your life!**

看！我們的新保險專案正在打折！它基本上涵蓋生活的所有層面。

5 **I wonder if my insurance company would cover our flight ticket after the flight was canceled due to the heavy snow.**

我在想，保險公司是否願意負擔我們因為大雪而被取消的機票費用。

6 **Dick, in case that you run into any kind of trouble during your fifteen days' trip in Europe, you'd better get insurance!**

迪克，為防你在十五天的歐洲之旅中遇到什麼困難，你還是保個險吧。

7 **Lynsey's new insurance company is famous for its credibility! So, I have several insurance cases under it!**

琳西新開的保險公司以信用良好而知名，所以我在那公司有好幾項保險。

8 **Gee, this person was detained for insurance scam!**

天啊！那個人因為詐領保險金而被羈押！

9 **Do you have insurance yet, Simon? If not, you can take our insurance set into consideration !**

你保險了嗎，賽門？如果還沒，你可以考慮我們的保險方案。

Part 9

出國旅行，

所有狀況跟任何人
都對答如流！

Unit 1

Appointments

——預約門診——

和每個人都聊得來 Track 045

加粗底線字：詳見「超萬用單字／句型」

A: Good morning, Doctor Owen's office. How can I help you?	早安，歐文醫師診所，有什麼我可以幫你的嗎？
B: Hi, I'd like to **make an appointment with** Doctor Owen.	你好，我想要預約跟歐文醫師的門診。
A: Ok, may I have your name?	好，麻煩您給我您的大名好嗎？
B: John Woosten.	約翰．伍斯頓。
A: Thank you, Mr. Woosten. What problem do you have?	謝謝，伍斯頓先生。您身體有什麼問題嗎？
B: I have severe diarrhea.	我有嚴重的腹瀉。
A: There's a slot available at 4:30 in the afternoon. Is this time ok for you?	好的，下午4點半有個空位，請問你這個時間可以嗎？
B: I'm sorry, I will still be at work. Is there any time available around 5:00?	不好意思，這個時間我還在工作，還有其他的時間嗎？
A: Yes, 5:30 is also available. I will **pencil you in** for 5:30. Is that ok?	有的，5點半也有空位，那我幫你預約5點半，可以嗎？
B: Great! That would be ok. Thank you for your help.	好，這個時間可以，謝謝你的幫忙。
A: My pleasure. We'll see you at 5:30 then.	不會，那麼5點半見。

B: Ok, bye. | Ok，掰。

超萬用單字／句型

▶ make an appointment with sb.

歐美人士預約醫院門診的話，通常使用「appointment」這個單字，而非一般餐廳訂位常用的「reservation」。除了 make an appointment with sb. 這個用法外，還可以用：fix an appointment with sb.，通常是指跟「人」預約。

❶ **A: Do you want to make an appointment?** → 請問您要預約嗎？
B: Yes, I do. → 是的。

❷ **A: Hello, I'd like to make an appointment with Dr. Sun at 5.**
→ 你好，我想預約 5:00，孫醫生。
B: Sorry, Dr. Sun will be available from 7.
→ 抱歉，孫醫生 7 點後才有空。

▶ pencil sb. in

pencil sb./sth. in= pencil in sb./sth. 暫定安排。當歐美人士在對話中有需要暫定或預先安排的情境，這時就以「pencil sb. in」、「pencil in sb.」來指會把你暫時安排進去，特別是指還沒完全確定的事，或確定的成員。

❶ **A: When is the company party?** → 公司尾牙在什麼時候？
B: Not sure yet. They'll pencil in the dates for the company party and confirm them later.
→ 還不確定。他們會先暫定尾牙日期後再確認。

❷ **A: I'll have to do a brief presentation for our group project.**
→ 我需要為我們的小組專案做個簡短的簡報。
B: Ok, I'll pencil you in for morning meeting.
→ Ok，我會把你安排進早會流程。

實用句型大補帖

1 **Mom, I'm stuck in traffic right now! Can you call the dentist clinic and cancel my appointment for me?**
媽，我現在困在車陣裡動彈不得！你能不能幫我打給牙醫診所取消預約？

2 **Gosh! Tim just got hit by a truck and was sent to the emergency room! He is going under the knife right now!**
天啊！提姆剛被卡車撞傷並且被緊急送進了急診室！他現在正在接受手術！

3 **Selphie, listen to me: you really should do something about your smoking addiction! I'll make an appointment for you today!**
賽爾菲，你聽我說！你真的需要治療一下你的菸癮！我今天就幫你預約！

4 **Elma's water just broke! We need to call the ambulance and send her to the emergency room right now!**
艾爾瑪的羊水破了！我們需要立刻叫救護車並且趕快把她送到急診室！

5 **Lisa is having a toothache and I'm calling the dentist for her. In my opinion, it might be the result of not brushing her teeth very often.**
麗莎正牙痛，我現在幫她打給牙醫師。我認為這應該是她不常刷牙所致。

6 **Hi, is it Ms. Lu? This is Dr. Lee's assistant calling. Your original appointment is rescheduled to Friday night at 7 p.m. Is that O.K. for you?**
嗨，請問是盧小姐嗎？我是李醫師的助理，您原先的預約已經被改到禮拜五晚上七點，請問這樣可以嗎？

7 **Tina, don't forget that you have an X-ray scan on Wednesday!**
堤娜，別忘了妳禮拜三要X光掃描檢查！

8 **My mom always says that the pain of giving birth to a child is excruciating and could be life-threatening without proper help!**
我媽總說生小孩很痛，且沒有完善的幫助的話可能危及生命！

9 **As long as you brush your teeth every day, you won't need to go to the dentist clinic so often!**
只要你每天刷牙，你就不用這麼常看牙醫了！

Unit 2

Out-patient Clinic

──門診──

和每個人都聊得來 *Track 046*

加粗底線字：詳見「超萬用單字／句型」

(At the counter)	（在櫃台）
A: Hi, We have an appointment at 10:30. Can we see the doctor now?	嗨！我們預約10:30，現在可以進去看醫生了嗎？
B: **Just a minute**, please.	請稍等一下。
(In the clinic)	（在診間）
A: Doctor, **what's wrong with my daughter?**	醫師，我女兒怎麼了？
B: She has the flu. Please monitor her temperature periodically.	她得了流感，請你幫她定時量體溫。
A: How often should I check her temperature?	那我該多久幫她量一次體溫呢？
B: Once every 5 hours.	每五小時一次。
A: What diet should I give her?	那她的飲食有需要注意的嗎？
B: She can only have liquid diet.	她只能吃流質食品。

A: When should I bring her for a return visit?	那我下次什麼時候帶她來複診？
B: After a week. You can make an appointment for next Thursday morning.	一週後。你可以先預約下星期四早上的門診。

超萬用單字／句型

▸What's wrong with sb.?

外國人在口語對話上常常對自己不理解的事或是疑惑對方的表現情形問一句 What's wrong? 來表示關心或關切。有時也只是簡短回覆對方的語句，疑問性地表達：「怎麼了？」

❶ **A: I'm so mad today!** → 我今天氣炸了！

B: What's wrong with you? → 你怎麼了？

❷ **A: I heard that Jamie cried this morning!**

→ 我聽說潔米早上哭了！

B: What's wrong with her? → 她發生什麼事？

▸Just a minute.

通常講電話或是在實際場合要對方稍待片刻時都用 Just a minute，它的意思近似於 Just a second，都可以當等一下，稍待的意思。

❶ **A: Hi, this is Tom Wang. Is Susie there?**

→ 嗨，我是王湯姆，請問蘇西在家嗎？

B: Just a minute! → 請稍待！

❷ **A: Lisa, the school bus is waiting!**

→ 麗莎，學校巴士在等妳唷！

B: Just a minute! → 馬上好。

實用句型大補帖

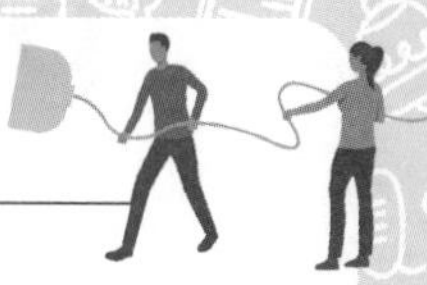

1 **Please lie on the surgery table and relax. The surgery will begin in just a few minutes.**
請平躺在手術台上並且放鬆。手術將於數分鐘內開始。

2 **Gosh, I'm having a really severe headache right now! Can you please take me to the hospital now?**
天啊！我現在頭很痛！你現在可不可以帶我去醫院？

3 **What's wrong? Can you figure out why so many people were injured and sent here?**
怎麼了？你知不知道為什麼那麼多人受傷並且被送來這裡？

4 **No matter what you do, stop trying to run away from the clinic!**
不管你做什麼，別再試圖從診所逃走！

5 **Please go to the second counter to your left for today's medicine, Ms. Liu.**
劉小姐，請至妳左邊數來第二個櫃台領取您今天的藥物。

6 **Where's Jessica? She should be in the psychiatrist's office by now starting her mental therapy.**
潔西卡人呢？她現在應該在心理醫生的辦公室接受心理治療啊。

7 **I really don't know what Elma was thinking. Going under a surgery and getting fake boobs is such a stupid idea!**
我真不知道愛爾瑪在想些什麼。接受手術做假胸部真是個蠢主意！

8 **Vivian is having a heart attack in the living room! Jamie is now calling 911.**
薇薇安在客廳心臟病發！潔米正打給119。

9 **Just a minute! Ok, the doctor is now available. Are you allergic to anything?**
稍等一下！好了，現在醫生有空了。你有對任何東西過敏嗎？

Unit 3

Power Outage

——停電——

和每個人都聊得來 Track 047

加粗底線字：詳見「超萬用單字／句型」

A: There's a power outage again!	又停電了！
B: I'd rather believe that it's just a temporary power outage.	我寧願相信這只是暫時的供電不足。
A: **Are you sure** it's just temporary?	你確定這只是暫時的嗎？
B: How should I know? What's going on with the super typhoon now?	我怎麼會知道？超級颱風現在怎麼樣了？
A: I have no idea. News about fallen trees and power outages is all that have been reported in the radio.	我不知道。目前為止，收音機只有吹倒大樹和停電的報導。
B: I guess major power outages have become a **common occurrence** in this area...	我想大停電在這一區已經成為家常便飯了……
A: True! The government and power company didn't even say anything about when the problem can be solved.	真的！政府和電力公司甚至完全沒提停電問題什麼時候解決。
B: Hear this! Power outage has stranded thousands of commuters on tracks and in sweltering tunnels.	聽聽這個！今天早上的一次停電使鐵軌上的上千名乘客被困在悶熱地道裡無法動彈。

A: Wow, their situation is even worse than ours. At least we're in our cozy home!	哇！他們的情況比我們更慘，至少停電時我們在舒適的家！

超萬用單字／句型

▶ Are you sure...

外國人在口語對話上常常會為了再次確認自己所接受到的訊息而反問 Are you sure 來確認對方真正的意思。如：

❶ **A: I'm going to compete with Lisa in the academic contest.**
→ 我要和麗莎進行學術競賽。

B: Are you sure you want to compete with that genius?
→ 你確定你想和那位天才競爭嗎？

❷ **A: Patrick's artwork won the heart of our teacher!**
→ 派翠克的美術作品贏得了老師的心！

B: Are you sure he made it by himself?
→ 你確定他是自己獨力完成的？

▶ common occurrence

歐美人士在說明此事「屢見不鮮」、「司空見慣」或「家常便飯」時，常會使用：common occurrence。通常用於指太常見以至於有點令人不悅的情境。有時會加上形容詞，如：terrible common occurrence。

❶ **A: There's been a car accident again in this area!**
→ 這區又發生車禍了！

B: Car accidents are a common occurrence around here.
→ 交通事故在這區屢見不鮮。

❷ **A: Another happily-ever-after ending?**
→ 又是個「從此以後幸福快樂」的結局？

B: That is a common occurrence in classic European fairly tales. → 這是在歐洲童話故事典型的現象。

實用句型大補帖

1. **Gosh! The sudden blackout in the city has prevented me from watching my favorite T.V. show and that bothers me!**
我的老天！突如其來的市區大停電讓我無法觀賞我最喜歡的電視節目，真讓我困擾。

2. **Mom! Where did you put the flashlight? I can't find it anywhere in the kitchen. Are you sure you didn't leave it in the living room?**
媽咪！你把手電筒放在哪了？我在廚房到處找遍了還是沒有找到。你確定你不是放在客廳嗎？

3. **Did you hear that there's a huge protest going on in front of the mayor's office due to the current power outage?**
你知道因為現在停電的關係，市長辦公室前有大型抗議嗎？

4. **Elma, could you please go and comfort your brother in the bedroom? It's so dark right now and I can't go upstairs during this blackout!**
艾爾瑪，你可以去臥室安撫一下你弟嗎？現在這麼黑，我無法在停電中走到樓上！

5. **Hey, that's the last candle stick we have! Light it up and use it wisely!**
嘿，那是我們最後一根蠟燭了！點燃後要好好使用啊！

6. **I heard that the electricity was out due to the destruction of the massive typhoon. I hope that everyone's O.K.**
我聽說斷電是因為強烈颱風所造成的破壞。我希望大家都沒事。

7. **I didn't finish my homework due to the blackout last night. How embarrassing! I wonder whether the teacher would believe me.**
因為昨晚停電，我沒有做完功課。好尷尬喔！我在想老師會不會相信我。

8. **Elle's family has their own solar energy generation machine and that's why the power outage didn't affect their lives.**
艾兒家有自己的太陽能發電機，那就是為什麼停電不會影響到他們的作息。

Unit 4

Asking for Directions

──問路──

和每個人都聊得來 Track 048

加粗底線字：詳見「超萬用單字／句型」

A: Oh, man! This guidebook is so lame! Excuse me, sir!	噢，天啊！這本旅遊指南真夠爛的！不好意思，先生！
B: Yes, what can I do for you?	是的，我能為你做什麼呢？
A: I'm looking for this restaurant around the train station. Do you know how to get there?	我正在找這間在火車站附近的餐廳，你知道要怎麼去嗎？
B: The restaurant on the guidebook?	在旅遊指南上的餐廳嗎？
A: Exactly! I really need some instructions; I have been walking around here for almost 20 minutes.	對！我真的需要指引，我在這裡繞了快20分鐘了。
B: Ok, let me **show you the way**. First, you have to go across that street, and turn right at the first corner. After that, turn left and go along the street…	Ok，讓我替你指路吧。首先，你要先跨越那條街，然後在第一個街角右轉，之後左轉然後沿著那條街……
A: Wait! I can't remember everything you've said; it's too complicated!	等等！我記不得你剛剛說的，太複雜了！
B: Ok, **let's put it this way:** first, you have got to find the train station. See that red building? Just go toward that direction. The red building is the train station.	Ok，讓我們這樣說吧，首先你必須找到火車站。看到那棟紅色建築了嗎？一直往那個方向走，那間紅色建築就是了。

A:	Oh! I kind of got the picture!	噢！我有點概念了！
B:	Good! And after that you can just turn right into the small lane, and you'll see the restaurant.	很好！在那之後你只要右轉進入那條小巷子，你就會看見餐廳了。

超萬用單字／句型

▶ show sb. the way

以口語詢問陌生人交通資訊時常使用此句型，如：「Can you show me the way?」而外國人也常用此句型表示只是道路資訊的意願，如：「Let me show you the way.」（讓我來帶路 / 指路吧！）

❶ **A: Excuse me, can you show me the way to the library?**
→ 不好意思，請問你知道哪裡可以找到圖書館嗎？

B: Go left and walk for ten minutes; you'll find it.
→ 左轉走十分鐘，你就會找到了。

❷ **A: Excuse me, do you know where to apply for jobs here?**
→ 不好意思，請問你知道在哪邊申請工作嗎？

B: Fill out the forms, and I'll show you the way.
→ 填完表格後，我會告訴你怎麼走。

▶ Let's put it this way,...

一般在對話中如果對方不懂你所說的意思時，外國人會再換句話說，把句子轉換成易懂的方式，意思近於中文裡的「這麼說好了」，一般用於句子的開頭。

❶ **A: What do you mean by saying Elle is a mean person?**
→ 你說艾兒是個刻薄的人是什麼意思？

B: Let's put it this way: she never helps others and criticizes people a lot. → 這麼說好了，她從不幫助人且經常批評別人。

❷ **A: Why do people say that the mayor is greedy?**
→ 為什麼人們說市長很貪婪？

B: Let's put it this way: he takes bribes often and uses the government budget for his advertisements!
→ 這麼說好了，他經常接受賄款，且挪用政府預算來做個人廣告！

實用句型大補帖

1

Excuse me, do you know where the Taipei Main Station is? And what's the quickest way to get there?

請問你知道台北火車站在哪裡嗎？然後怎樣可以最快到那裡？

2

Turn left on Cooper road and keep walking for three blocks and you will find the Spring department store on your left!

在庫柏路左轉然後持續走三個街區，你將會發現春天百貨公司就在你的左手邊！

3

Go two blocks straight and you will find a parking lot.

向前直走兩個街區你會看到停車場。

4

Let's put it this way: when you see a red brick building turn left and keep walking for about ten minutes, then you will find the book store.

這麼說好了，當你看到一棟磚紅色的建築就往左轉繼續走大概十分鐘，你就會找到那家書店了。

5

According to the map that I downloaded from the Internet, the Chinese restaurant should be right here. But we see no signs of it; perhaps the restaurant was shut down a long time ago.

根據我從網路上下載的地圖，那間中國餐廳應該就在這裡。但我們看不到任何跡象，也許餐廳很久以前已經關閉了。

6

I heard that Cindy got lost in the mountains, but luckily she met other mountain climbers and they showed her the way.

聽說辛蒂在山裡迷路，不過幸好她遇到其它的登山客幫她指路。

7

Where can I find a nice and fancy restaurant in the city? I didn't bring my car today so I'm looking for a restaurant nearby my office.

在市區哪裡可以找到一家好吃又時髦的餐廳？我今天沒開車所以我想找一家離辦公室近的餐廳。

8

How did you get here in such a short time?

你是怎麼在短時間內到達這的？

Unit 5

Leak

——漏水——

和每個人都聊得來 Track 049

加粗底線字：詳見「超萬用單字／句型」

A: Good afternoon, YW Plumbing. This is Peterson.	午安，YW水電公司您好，我是彼得森。
B: Hi, I've got a plumbing problem and really need it to be fixed as soon as possible. Is there anyone available to **do a house call** right now?	嗨，我有水管漏水問題，希望你們能儘快派人來修。有人現在可以過來嗎？
A: Can you tell me what the problem is?	可以告訴我您的問題嗎？
B: It's the pipe in the kitchen. It's leaking.	是廚房的水管，正在漏水。
A: Has this problem been going on for a long time?	這個問題持續很久了嗎？
B: Not for a long time. It just happened an hour ago.	不會很久，大約1小時前開始。
A: Alright. Please hold on for a second.	好的，請稍等一下。
(1 minute later)	（1分鐘後）

A: Hi, all our plumbers are out now. Is it ok if someone comes over at 6:30?	您好，目前所有水電工都外派中。大約6:30到府服務可以嗎？
B: The soonest is 4 hours later? **Nonsense!**	最快要4小時後？胡扯吧！

超萬用單字／句型

▸ Nonsense!

外國人在口語對話上如果遇到自己不同意的是或是想要極力反駁，意思類似中文的「胡說」或是「亂講」，如：

❶ **A: I saw a pig flying in the sky yesterday!**
→ 我昨天看到一隻豬在天上飛！

B: Nonsense! → 胡說！

❷ **A: Did you know that Amy just got married with Horace?**
→ 你知道艾咪剛和荷瑞斯結婚了嗎？

B: Nonsense! → 亂講！

▸ do a house call

早期歐美的醫師經常到病患家出診，house call 原意是指醫師「出診」。不過經過一段時間後，house call 卻引申出「到府服務」的意思。

❶ **A: My mom gave birth to my little brother at home!**
→ 我媽在家裡生下了我的小弟。

B: So Dr. Louis did a house call for her?
→ 所以路易醫生到你們家出診嗎？

❷ **A: Hi. My pipe keeps leaking; can anyone do a house call now?**
→ 嗨，我的水管一直漏，現在可以派人到府服務嗎？

B: Ok, will arrive in 10 minutes.
→ Ok，會在 10 分鐘內抵達。

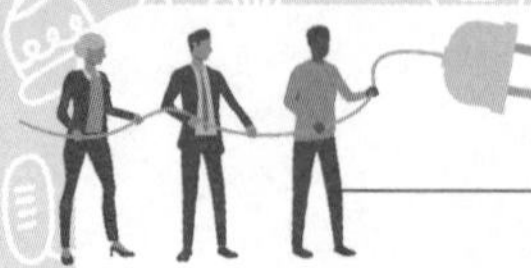

實用句型大補帖

1 **Mom, the dripping faucet in our bathroom is creating a waterfall!**
媽，浴室漏水的水龍頭已經在廁所形成瀑布了！

2 **My brother broke our kitchen faucet when he was playing with water this morning. I'll have to fix it before mom gets back!**
我弟弟今天早上玩水時弄壞了廚房的水龍頭，我必須要在我媽回來前修好！

3 **As a result of my leaking faucet, I paid two thousand Dollars for my water usage this month.**
因為我的水龍頭漏水，我這個月付了兩千元水費。

4 **The leaking in the high school's water supply system led to a serious hygiene problem.**
高中的供水系統漏水造成了嚴重的衛生問題。

5 **Kate didn't break the pipe; it was damaged during the earthquake!**
凱特沒有弄壞水管啦！它是在地震中壞的！

6 **Please find someone to help me here! I can't stop the water from coming out of my toilet.**
拜託找人來幫幫我！我無法阻止水從馬桶溢出！

7 **The water shortage in our village is a result of the massive leaking of the main pipe underground.**
我們村裡的水源短缺是由於地下水管主幹大量漏水導致。

8 **Elma, can you do something to cut off the water supply?**
愛爾瑪，你能不能切斷水源？

9 **I told you to fix your faucet last week and you wouldn't listen! Now your house is full of water.**
我上禮拜就叫你去修理水龍頭，但你不聽！現在你家整個都是水。

Unit 6

Air Conditioner

——空調——

和每個人都聊得來 Track 050

加粗底線字：詳見「超萬用單字／句型」

A: Oh! Gosh! It feels like a stove in here! Why don't we turn on the air conditioner?	噢！天啊！這裡是火爐吧！我們為什麼不開冷氣啊？
B: Well, look around! Do you see the AC?	嗯，看看四周，你有看到冷氣嗎？
A: Hey, don't tell me that you haven't installed the AC!	嘿！不要告訴我你一直沒裝冷氣！
B: I haven't!	我一直沒裝啊！
A: Holy cow! How can you survive this hot summer?	老天爺喔！你怎麼度過這個超熱的夏天啊？
B: **No matter how** hot it may be, I can just live on with electric fans. That's enough.	不管有多熱，我可以只靠電風扇。這樣就夠了。
A: For God's sake, stop persuading me to use only electric fans!	看在老天的份上，不要再說服我只用電風扇了！
B: Wow, buddy! You really know me well!	哇，老兄！你真懂我耶！
A: Come on! If you can't be called an environmentalist, who can?	拜託！如果你不能被稱作環保人士，那就沒人是環保人士了！

B: Yeah! **As far as I'm concerned,** the AC is another root for "global warming"...

是啊！就我所知，冷氣也算是另一個「全球暖化」的元兇喔……

超萬用單字／句型

▶no matter how...

「無論……」的意思，通常用於表達條件或特殊情況。

❶ **A: I thought you were interested in that Spanish class. Why haven't you been show up recently?**

→ 我以為你對那堂西班牙文課很有興趣呢，為什麼你最近都沒出現？

B: No matter how hard I tried, I can't manage to speak Spanish well so I gave up.

→ 不管我怎麼努力，我都無法把西班牙文說得很好，所以我放棄了。

❷ **A: He is a very handsome and attractive man. Does he already have someone?**

→ 他真的是個又帥又有魅力的男人，他有女朋友了嗎？

B: Forget it! He's married. No matter how beautiful you are, it's impossible for you to be his girlfriend.

→ 算了吧！他已經結婚了，不管妳有多美麗都不可能當他的女朋友。

▶As far as one is concerned, ...

直翻成中文為：就我所關心的程度而言，意近似於「就我所知」。通常用於較正式的發言場合或較認真的言論。

❶ **A: Do you know how to reduce the number of cockroaches in my room?** → 你知道怎麼減少我房間裡蟑螂的數量嗎？

B: As far as I am concerned, pouring soap water is very useful. → 就我所知，灑一些肥皂水很有用。

❷ **A: Which restaurant should we go to for dinner?**

→ 我們晚餐應該去哪家餐廳？

B: As far as I am concerned, the one at the corner is the best.

→ 就我所知，轉角那家最好吃。

實用句型大補帖

1 **I really want to turn on the air conditioner but it has been broken for three days.**
我實在很想開冷氣，可是它已經壞了三天。

2 **Based on the news this morning, I suggest we had better reduce the hours of using the air conditioner.**
基於今天早上的新聞，我建議我們最好減少使用冷氣的時數。

3 **No matter how hot it is, you shouldn't turn on every air conditioner in the house if you are only staying in your own room.**
不管有多熱，如果你只待在自己房間裡，就不應該把家裡每台冷氣都打開。

4 **The electricity is included in the rent, so feel free to turn on the AC so long as you feel hot or muggy.**
電費已經包含在房租了，所以只要你覺得悶熱就可以自由開冷氣。

5 **As far as I am concerned, if you put a glass of water in the office with the air conditioner on, you'll be less likely to have a headache.**
就我所知，如果在辦公室冷氣房裡放一杯水，頭痛的機率會降低。

6 **It's as hot as hell here! I thought the air conditioner was already fixed. Why don't you adjust the room temperature to something more comfortable?**
這裡像地獄一樣，我以為冷氣已經修好了。你為什麼不把室內溫度調得舒適一點？

7 **I don't like my new spot in the office; it's in the corner where the cool air from the air conditioner can't reach at all.**
我不喜歡辦公室的新座位，在角落邊根本吹不到冷氣。

8 **If you are not yet going to sleep, then don't turn on the air conditioner.**
如果你還沒有要睡覺就不要開冷氣。

Unit 7

Renting an Apartment

—租屋—

和每個人都聊得來 *Track 051*

加粗底線字：詳見「超萬用單字／句型」

A: Hello, I saw your ad on the website.	我在網站上看到你們的廣告。
B: What kind of room are you looking for?	請問你在找什麼樣的房間？
A: I am looking for a one-bedroom apartment. Do you have any vacancies?	我在找一間單人床公寓。你有任何空房嗎？
B: Yes, it's furnished. Do you want to see the house?	有，而且有附傢俱。要看一下房子嗎？
A: Sure. Is it ok to see the house at 3 tomorrow? **For your convenience,** can we exchange phone numbers?	當然好。明天3點OK嗎？為了方便起見，我們交換一下電話號碼好嗎？
(At the apartment for rent)	（在出租公寓）
B: It's near the subway station here, and the neighborhood is quiet.	這裡離地鐵站很近，而且周圍很安靜。
A: Wow, seems great! What's the rent, and what is the duration of the lease?	哇，感覺很棒！租屋合約請問要簽約多久呢？
B: The rent is 1,000 dollars per month, utilities excluded. The lease is valid for 5 years.	租金每個月1,000元，不含水電，另外租約是5年。

(At the café)	（在咖啡廳）
B: Did you rent the apartment you saw yesterday?	妳租了昨天去看的公寓嗎？
A: The rent is super expensive, and **what's worse**, the lease duration is 5 years,which is too long!	租金極貴，更糟的是，租約要五年，超長的！

超萬用單字／句型

▶ What's worse,...

外國人常在描述事情的嚴重程度時，在最糟糕、最不能忍受的情況前加上這一句來強調狀況有多糟。如：

❶ **A: Why are you in a hurry?** → 你為什麼這麼趕？

B: I woke up late, and I couldn't find my wallet; what's worse, I'm running out of time for the meeting. → 我起得太晚了，又找不到錢包，更糟的是我已經快趕不上開會的時間了。

❷ **A: Why didn't you buy that skirt?** → 妳為什麼沒買那件裙子？

B: That skirt is not suitable for me, and the color is ugly; what's worse, it's too expensive!

→ 那件裙子並不適合我，而且顏色很醜，更糟的是它太貴了！

▶ for your convenience

外國人常在禮貌上會使用這句話，意思相當於「為了方便起見」。如：

❶ **A: I don't have your e-mail address.** → 我沒有你的電子信箱。

B: Oh, I forget! For your convenience, I think I can also give you my cell phone number.

→ 噢，我忘了！為了方便起見，我想我也可以留我的手機號碼給你。

❷ **A: Do you know how to contact Dr. Hou?**

→ 你知道如何聯絡上侯博士嗎？

B: Sure, I have her e-mail address. I can also give you her office's number for your convenience. → 當然，我有她的電子信箱。為了方便起見我也可以給你她辦公室的電話。

實用句型大補帖

1
I want to move out from the dormitory because it's too cramped, and what's worse, there's no air conditioner.
我想搬離宿舍，因為它空間太狹窄了，更糟的是，它沒有冷氣。

2
Do you have any friend who wants to rent a new apartment recently?
你有沒有任何朋友最近想要租房子的？

3
For your convenience, I can give you my phone number so that you can contact me whenever you want to visit the apartment.
方便起見，我可以給你我的電話，如此一來當你想看公寓時就可以隨時聯絡得到我。

4
The apartment we just visited yesterday was not bad; I will rent it on the condition that the owner allows me to keep my dog there.
昨天我們看過的那間公寓還不錯，只要房東能讓我養狗我就會租下它。

5
Alice is looking for a new apartment and her ideal budget rent is $150 per month.
艾莉絲正在找新公寓，然後她的房租預算是每月150元。

6
The sink of my current apartment has been broken for at least a month already and I can't get hold of the owner. I really don't know whether I should fix it by myself or not.
我現在住處的洗手台已經壞了至少一個月，然後我又連絡不到房東，真不知道我能不能自己修。

7
I really like my new apartment that I just rented last month.
我真的很喜歡上個月才租下來的新公寓。

8
The reason Emma told you not to bargain with the owner for the rent is that the price is actually very reasonable.
艾瑪要妳別跟房東在房租上討價還價的理由是那個價格已經很合理了。

9
It really bothers me that my new roommate always brings a lot of friends to our apartment without notifying me.
室友總是帶很多朋友回我們的住處卻又不告知我，讓我覺得很困擾。

Unit 8

Traffic Jam

——塞車——

和每個人都聊得來 Track 052

加粗底線字：詳見「超萬用單字／句型」

A: Where is Thomas? The meeting is starting in 5 minutes!	湯瑪士在哪？會議5分鐘後就要開始了！
B: Well, I have no idea. Isn't he the one who is responsible for the presentation?	嗯，我也不知道。他不是要負責今天的簡報嗎？
A: Yep! That's why we need him to be here right now.	是啊！所以他應該現在就要在這裡了！
B: Oh, ok, I will call him now.	噢，好吧，我現在打給他。
(after the call)	（打了電話後）
A: What did he say? Will he get here in time?	他說什麼？他可以及時抵達吧？
B: Well, I couldn't reach him. No one answered the phone.	嗯……連絡不上他，沒人接聽。
A: Damn! We're all done, if he can't come before the presentation!	糟了！如果他不能在簡報前到達，我們就都完蛋了！
B: I've heard on the news today that commuters heading toward this area are stuck in traffic.	我聽到新聞說前往本區的通勤者都塞在路上。

A: God! **Could you do me a favor?** Ask him to take the subway!	啊！你可以幫我個忙嗎？叫他搭地鐵來！
B: Wait! Thomas is calling! (30 seconds later...) He **went to the toilet** downstairs and is coming now!	等等！湯瑪士回電了！（30秒後……）他剛去樓下上廁所，現在正要過來了。

超萬用單字／句型

▶Could you do me a favor?

請別人幫忙時常會講到這句話，又可說 Could (Would) you give me a hand? 或 May I ask a favor of you? 助動詞 could (would) 會比 can 來得更客氣、禮貌。

❶ **A: Excuse me. Could you do me a favor?**
→ 不好意思，您能否幫我一個忙？
B: Sure. What do you need? → 當然好，你需要些什麼呢？

❷ **A: Sophie, could you do me a favor?**
→ 蘇菲，您能幫我一個忙嗎？
B: I would like to, but I have a meeting in 5 minutes.
→ 我很樂意，但是我再過五分鐘就要開會了……。

▶go to the toilet

toilet 有「廁所、馬桶」的意思，在此指的是「馬桶」。請注意 go to the toilet 是較不禮貌的說法，應用較委婉的說法：go to restroom / washroom / bathroom。

❶ **A: Mommy, I need to go to the toilet.** → 媽咪，我要上廁所。
B: OK. I'll wait right here until you're done.
→ 好，我在這裡等你上完廁所。

❷ **A: Can I go to the toilet?** → 我可以去上廁所嗎？
B: Sure! → 當然可以！

實用句型大補帖

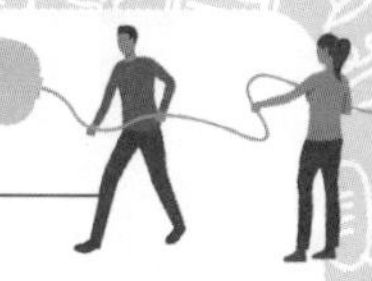

1 **I'm sorry. I am stuck in a traffic jam. Could you do me a favor and tell the host that I'll be a little late?**
對不起，路上塞車，你可以幫我跟主辦人說我會晚點到嗎？

2 **You should leave home early, or you will be trapped in the traffic jam.**
你應該要早點出門，不然很容易塞車喔！

3 **There seems to be an accident ahead, so we are stuck in traffic.**
前面好像發生車禍，所以我們塞在車陣中。

4 **If I am still stuck in the traffic jam, I will miss the 10 a.m. meeting.**
再這樣塞車下去，我就趕不上十點的會議了。

5 **I think there will be heavy traffic on the highway during the five-day holiday. Should we set off early to avoid the traffic jam?**
接下來有五天連假，我想到時候高速公路一定會大塞車！我們要不要提早出發避開車潮？

6 **Traffic police officers are dispatched to control and manage the traffic flow, but the traffic jams can't be solved right away .**
雖然有交通警察管制車流量，但也沒辦法立刻解決塞車的問題……。

7 **Being stuck in a traffic jam is common at the rush hour. Let's take the MRT.**
上下班等尖峰時刻最容易塞車了，我們搭捷運吧！

8 **When will the traffic jam be over? I really need to go to the toilet.**
到底還要塞多久啊？我想上廁所！

9 **I tried to find another route to escape the traffic jam, but in vain .**
我試著找另一條能避開塞車的路線，但沒找到。

10 **What do you do during traffic jams?**
塞車的時候你都做些什麼？

11 **Ariel was on her way to the airport when she hit a serious traffic jam.**
艾莉兒去機場的途中遇上大塞車。

12 **She was late for the interview because of a traffic jam.**
因為塞車，所以她面試遲到了。

13 **The government has decided to investigate the main cause of the traffic jams.**
政府決定調查交通阻塞的主因。

Unit 9

Traffic Violation

——交通違規——

和每個人都聊得來 Track 053

加粗底線字：詳見「超萬用單字／句型」

A: Have you heard what happened to Daniel?	你有聽到有關丹尼爾的事嗎？
B: Why? He's not in the office today. Is he sick?	為什麼這麼問？他今天沒來辦公室。他生病了嗎？
A: Nope! He's in the hospital; they said he **almost died** on the spot.	才不是！他現在住院；他們說他昨天差點死在現場。
B: Sounds terrible! What exactly happened to him?	聽起來很慘！他到底發生了什麼事啊？
A: Well, he was in a car crash last night.	嗯，他昨晚發生車禍。
B: But he never speeds. I've never seen him with any tickets for any violations.	可是他從不超速的，我根本沒看過他拿到任何一張違規罰單。
A: It is said that the accident was caused **under the influence of alcohol**.	聽說昨天的車禍是酒駕造成的。
B: What? You mean that Daniel drunk drove last night?	什麼？你說丹尼爾酒駕？

A: No, it was another driver who ran into Daniel's car and caused the accident.	不是，是撞丹尼爾的駕駛酒駕，並引發了這起車禍事故。
B: They should get that person's license revoked!	他們真應該永遠吊銷那個人的駕照！

超萬用單字／句型

▸ sb. almost died...

I almost died. 是更戲劇性、誇張地表達心中對某事物的看法。I almost died 後面可接 V-ing。如：

❶ **A: Hey, have you seen this picture?**
→ 嘿，你有看過這張照片嗎？

B: Yeah, when I saw this picture I almost died laughing!
→ 有啊，我看到的時候差點笑死。

❷ **A: I was incredibly scared last night. I almost died.**
→ 我昨晚差點被嚇死了。

B: What happened? → 發生了什麼事啊？

▸ under the influence of

「under the influence of + 人／事／物」表示在某人／事／物的影響下，因此 drive under the influence of alcohol ＝在酒的影響下開車，就是酒駕！ Drunk driving 也是酒駕的意思。

❶ **A: Don't drive under the influence of alcohol.** → 別酒駕！

B: I am stone sober. → 我清醒得很。

❷ **A: He was arrested for driving under the influence of alcohol.**
→ 他因為酒駕被補。

B: I told him not to drink so much.
→ 我告訴過他別喝那麼多的。

實用句型大補帖

1 **I received a traffic ticket for running a red light.**
我因為闖紅燈收到一張罰單。

2 **The driver was pulled over by a police officer for speeding on the freeway.**
駕駛人因在高速公路超速而遭警察攔下。

3 **What is the maximum speed limit on this highway?**
這條高速公路的最高速限是多少？

4 **An old man who was hit by a teenager running a red light almost died.**
那位因青少年闖紅燈被撞的老人差點喪命。

5 **Why did you run the red light? Don't you know it is dangerous?**
為什麼你要闖紅燈？你不知道這樣很危險嗎？

6 **The traffic police will clamp down on speeders and red light runners.**
交通警察將加強取締超速及闖紅燈的駕駛人。

7 **The government has decided to set up more video cameras at intersections to capture images of vehicles committing traffic violations.**
政府已決定在十字路口設置更多監測攝影機，以便拍下違反交通規則的車輛。

8 **You will be fined if you exceed the speed limit by more than 50km per hour.**
如果你的時速超過五十公里，就會被罰鍰。

9 **If you violate the speed limit, run a red light and drive under the influence of alcohol, you will have your driver's license revoked/suspended.**
如果你超速、闖紅燈又酒駕，你的駕照將被吊銷。

10 **You are fined for two reasons. One is running a red light and the other is speeding.**
你會被罰錢有二個原因，一個是闖紅燈，另一個是超速。

11 **I promise I won't speed again. Could you please forgive me this time?**
我保證不再超速了，這次可以請你原諒我嗎？

Part 10

歡慶節日，

搞懂節日文化、和任何人
都可以相約歡慶節日！

Unit 1

Chinese New Year

──農曆新年──

和每個人都聊得來 Track 054

加粗底線字：詳見「超萬用單字／句型」

A: Hey! How was your Chinese new year?	嗨！農曆新年過的如何？
B: Nothing special, **I mean** I always got to spent time with my whole family as usual.	沒什麼特別的。我是說就跟之前一樣，我都跟家人在一起。
A: What did you guys do?	你們都做了些什麼？
B: We played mahjong together; I really cleaned up this year! You?	我們一起打麻將，今年真的是大撈一筆呢！你呢？
A: We set off firecrackers on the first day of Chinese New Year.	我們在春節第一天會使用鞭炮。
B: Yeah, I know! People believe that firecrackers can drive the Nien monster away.	對，我知道！大家相信鞭炮會把年獸趕走。
A: Exactly! As the tradition goes, we went to visit all our relatives.	按照傳統我們到處去親戚家拜年。
B: Did you have a great time with them? **By the way**, did you have great food there?	你在親戚家開心嗎？對了，你有在他們家吃到美食嗎？

A: The food was spectacular! My aunt makes the best dumplings.	食物超讚的！我的伯母包的餃子最棒了。
B: Wow! Those are my favorite, too! My grandma says that eating dumplings can make you rich and prosperous.	哇！那也是我最愛吃的！我的祖母說，吃餃子可以財富滾滾、好運旺旺來。

超萬用單字／句型

▶ I mean...

此句可解釋為「我的意思是……。」是一種用來連接句子的助詞，常用在當對方不明白自己的意思，而需要多加說明時。亦可用來表示辯解，希望對方能清楚了解自己的意思，而不至於產生誤解時使用。此句前方通常為主要的話題，並使用I mean來連接補充的話題。

❶ **A: Sorry, I don't quite understand what you mean by that.**
→ 抱歉，我並不是很明白你那樣是什麼意思。
B: Well, I mean this equation should be solved like this.
→ 嗯，我是說這個算式應該這樣算。

❷ **A: Why are you nervous? I mean, you will be fine, so don't worry!** → 你為什麼緊張？我的意思是說你會沒事的，所以別擔心。
B: Well, thank you for saying that. → 嗯，謝謝你這麼說。

▶ By the way,...

此句可譯為另外、此外的，是一種用來轉換話題的句型片語。也可以用來當作補充話題或是提醒他人之意。

❶ **A: I would like to order this. By the way, can I also get a coke?** → 我想點這一個。另外，我可以再要一杯可樂嗎？
B: Alright, sir. → 沒問題，先生。

❷ **A: Oh, by the way, don't forget to bring the file with you!**
→ 噢，對了！別忘了帶那份資料。
B: Ok, I will. → 好的，我會記得的。

實用句型大補帖

1 Happy Chinese New Year! Do you have any plans for the break?
新年快樂！你假期有什麼安排嗎？

2 Chinese New Year is my favorite festival of the year. I mean, there are many great foods, and you can meet many people.
農曆新年是我一年中最喜歡的節日。我是指，有很多很棒的食物又可以見到很多人。

3 Look at those children. I bet they can't wait to get the red envelopes.
看看那些孩子們，我敢說他們一定等不及要領紅包了。

4 Hey guys, please get ready soon! We are going to grandma's house. Don't make her wait, ok?
嘿！大夥，趕快準備吧！我們要去外婆家了。別讓她等，好嗎？

5 In fact, I don't really like to go out during the New Year, because many stores are usually closed for the break. Besides, sometimes you will find that many places are full of people.
其實我不是很喜歡在新年出門，因為通常許多店家也都因為休假關門。除此之外，有的時候你又會發現很多地方擠滿了人。

6 The gathering feast is quite a significant event of the Chinese New Year.
年夜飯在農曆新年裡可以說是重頭戲。

7 I want to buy some new clothes! Haven't you heard that Chinese New Year is a time for a new start? By the way, everything is on sale now, too.
我想去買些新衣服！你沒聽過農曆新年就是要除舊佈新嗎？另外，現在也在大特價。

8 Hey let's get some couplets. I think it is better to decorate the house with things that are related to the New Year.
嘿，我們去買些春聯吧。我覺得還是要把家裡布置得有年節氣氛一點會比較好。

9 We'd better leave early tomorrow. The traffic has been quite jammed since yesterday, because the holiday is nearly over.
我們明天最好提早離開吧，路上從昨天開始就已經很塞了，因為假期快要結束了。

10 Why don't we play cards? Finally everyone is here.
不如我們來打牌吧？大家好不容易都在這。

Unit 2

Valentine's Day

——情人節——

和每個人都聊得來 Track 055

加粗底線字：詳見「超萬用單字／句型」

A: Here are some flowers, my love. Happy Valentine's Day!	親愛的，送妳一些花。情人節快樂！
B: Those are so beautiful! They smell lovely. Thank you.	這些花真漂亮！真好聞，謝謝你。
A: This is to let you know that I still love you after all these years. **Don't you think** our love is God-blessed?	送妳這些花是想讓妳知道，過了這麼多年我依然很愛妳。妳不覺得我們的愛是受到祝福的嗎？
B: How sweet! I knew that there would be ups and downs when I married you. But through it all, you've always been my love, too.	你這麼說真好！嫁你的時候我就知道生活會有快樂會有悲傷，但是，一路走過來，你也一直是我最心愛的人。
A: I want to thank you for your kindness and patience. And most of all, you've always been there for me.	我要感謝妳對我的好、對我的耐心。最重要的是，妳一直守護在我身邊。
B: I'd do everything for you, you know that. Maybe you didn't realize it, but you made every day a joyous moment and a happy occasion for me.	我願意為你做任何事情，你知道的。也許你沒有意識到，可是你讓我每一天都變得很開心、很幸福。
A: I'm so glad that we met each other.	我很高興我們遇到了彼此。

B: I have something for you, too, my dear! **I'm pretty sure** that you'll love it!	我也有東西要給你，親愛的！我相信你會愛死這個禮物！
A: Wow! The tickets for the film I really want to see in the cinema with you! Love you, darling!	哇！是我一直想跟妳去看的那部片的電影票耶！親愛的，我愛妳！

超萬用單字／句型

▶ I am pretty sure...

這句片語意為「我非常確定」，具有肯定以及確信之意。通常用在與對方搭話或是回應他人的時候。

❶ **A: I am pretty sure the answer for this question is A.**
→ 我非常確定這題的答案是 A。
B: Really? → 真的嗎？

❷ **A: I am pretty sure I saw Tom at the bus stop yesterday.**
→ 我很確定我昨天在公車站看到湯姆。
B: Really! I haven't seen him for a while.
→ 真的嘛！我有一陣子沒看到他了。

▶ Don't you think...?

這是一句疑問句的開頭，可以解釋為「你不這麼認為嗎？」後方可接欲詢問對方的事情。也可以當作一句反問句來詢問對方的意見使用。

❶ **A: Don't you think the pink shirt looks better than the blue one?** → 你不覺得粉紅色的那件比藍色的那件看起來好多了嗎？
B: But I like blue more. → 不過我比較喜歡藍色。

❷ **A: Don't you think it will be better for you to talk to Kate?**
→ 你不覺得你應該和凱特談談會比較好嗎？
B: Ok, I will. → 好啦，我會的。

實用句型大補帖

1 **Happy Valentine's! I already made a reservation at your favorite restaurant.**
情人節快樂！我預約好你最喜歡的餐廳了。

2 **God, I really love this present. You are so sweet, honey!**
天哪，我真的很喜歡這個禮物。你真是太貼心，親愛的！

3 **I am pretty sure every nice restaurant is full because of Valentine's Day. If you don't make early reservations, usually you won't be able to get in.**
我很確定所有優質餐廳都會因為情人節而客滿。如果你不早點訂位通常都進不去。

4 **Look at all those heart-shaped chocolates! They are so cute and sweet. I bet girls are crazy about them.**
看看那些心型的巧克力！它們真是甜美又可愛，我敢說女孩一定為它們感到瘋狂。

5 **Actually I still don't know why Teddy bears have anything to do with Valentine's Day, but they do look pretty cute.**
其實我還是不知道為什麼泰迪熊娃娃會跟情人節有關連。不過它看起來的確相當可愛。

6 **Look at the people on the street. So many couples are holding hands!**
看看那些走在街上的人，好多牽著手的情侶！

7 **Actually I don't really like to go out on Valentine's Day. We usually stay at our place, order a pizza and watch a DVD together.**
其實我並不是很喜歡在情人節那天出門。我們通常會待在家裡，訂個披薩然後一起看個DVD。

8 **Today is our first Valentine's Day together! Don't you think we should do something special to celebrate it together?**
今天是我們的第一個情人節！你不覺得我們應該想一些特別的方式來慶祝一下嗎？

9 **You know if you guys are together for a while, you probably won't take Valentine's Day so seriously.**
你知道如果你們已經在一起一段時間了，你大概就不會太認真看待情人節。

Unit 3

Father's/Mother's Day

—父親/母親節—

和每個人都聊得來 Track 056

加粗底線字：詳見「超萬用單字／句型」

A: Hi, young lady. How may I help you?	嗨，小女孩。我能為妳做些什麼嗎？
B: Well…I'm looking for a Father's Day's gift.	嗯……我想找父親節禮物。
A: Ok! **What do you think of** getting your father a new wallet?	Ok！妳覺得送給妳爸一個新皮夾怎麼樣？
B: Hmm. How much is that black wallet?	嗯。那個黑色皮夾多少錢呢？
A: Oh, it's only $20.95.	噢，這只要20.95元。
B: Really? That's great! I think my father will like the design on the outside!	真的嗎？太好了！我想我爸會喜歡這個皮夾上面的設計！
A: It's on sale now, so it's only $20.95. Want anything else?	它在特價中，只要20.95元。還有要其他東西嗎？
B: Please just give me this one, and here you go.	麻煩給我這個皮夾就好了，這是20.95元。
(At home)	（在家裡）

A: Hey, why does my little girl keep standing here behind Daddy?	嘿，爹地的小女孩為什麼一直站在爹地身後呢？
B: Dad, it's for you, and **I just want to say**: "I love you!"	爹地，這是給你的，然後我只想說：「我愛你！」

超萬用單字／句型

▸ What do you think of...?

這句通常解釋為「你認為……。」是一句用來詢問他人意見的常用句。句型中所接的主句為欲詢問對方的內容。主詞的內容可以是簡單的物品或人名等單字，另外也可以是一整句的進行式動作。

❶ **A: What do you think of going to Chicago this summer?**
→ 你覺得這個夏天去芝加哥怎麼樣？
B: That will be great! → 那真是太棒了！

❷ **A: What do you think of this shirt? I'm not sure if I should buy it or not.** → 你認為這件衣服怎麼樣？我不知道該不該買下來。
B: Well, it is not bad, I think. → 嗯，我覺得還不錯。

▸ I just want to say...

這句可以翻譯為「我是想說……。」是一句平時常用的搭話語，後方只要直接接上想說的話，就可以使用在一般對話中，輕鬆與人搭話交談。

❶ **A: I just want to say that you have done a great job in the competition.** → 我只是想說你在比賽中的表現真的很出色。
B: Thank you so much! → 謝謝你的讚美！

❷ **A: I just want to say that I am sorry for the misunderstanding.**
→ 我只想說我對於這次的誤會感到很抱歉。
B: It's ok, I understand.
→ 沒關係，我可以理解。

實用句型大補帖

1 **Do you remember tomorrow is Mother's Day? What are we going to do for Mom?**
你記得明天是母親節嗎？我們要替媽媽準備什麼？

2 **What do you think of this purse? Do you think she will like it as her Mother's Day gift?**
你覺得這個皮包怎麼樣？你覺得她會喜歡它當母親節禮物嗎？

3 **I think we can get a new belt for Dad as his Father's Day present. He said his belt was kind of broken and he needed a new one.**
我覺得我們可以買條新的皮帶當作父親節禮物。他之前說過他的皮帶有點舊需要換新了。

4 **Look at those cakes. They look so delicious! They're on sale for Mother's Day. Isn't it nice?**
看那些蛋糕，看起來好好吃！現在正在做母親節特惠呢，不覺得超讚的嗎？

5 **Well, compared to buying flowers as a present for my parents, I would rather buy a cake, because you can at least share it with everyone!**
嗯，比起買花給我的父母當禮物，我寧願買蛋糕，因為至少你可以和大家分享！

6 **Hey, Dad! I got a present for you; hope you will like it. And happy Father's Day!**
嘿，老爸！我有個禮物要給你，希望你會喜歡。還有父親節快樂！

7 **Hey, Mom, this is your gift for Mother's Day. Open it and have a look !**
嘿，媽！這是你的母親節禮物。趕快打開來看看吧！

8 **What do you usually buy for your parents on Mother's Day and Father's Day?**
你通常都會送你父母什麼當母親節和父親節禮物？

9 **I just want to say that you are the most wonderful father in the world!**
我只是想說你是世界上最棒的爸爸！

Unit 4

Birthday Party

——生日派對——

和每個人都聊得來 Track 057

加粗底線字：詳見「超萬用單字／句型」

A: What are you up to?	你最近在忙些什麼？
B: I am listening to the songs of a cool band. They rock!	我在聽一個很酷的樂團的歌。他們超讚！
A: Cool! Do you know what day is today?	酷耶！那你知道今天是幾號嗎？
B: No. I don't have a clue.	不，我一點都不清楚。
A: Today is June 24th, my birthday.	今天是6月24日，我的生日。
B: Will you have a party later?	你待會要舉辦一個生日派對嗎？
A: Of course, it's a custom for me. Will you come?	當然，每年我生日的時候都要舉辦生日派對。你會來吧？
B: You bet.	當然。
(At the birthday party)	（生日派對上）
B: Happy birthday! I got this for you!	生日快樂！我幫你帶了這個！

A: Cool! A CD! **Help yourself!**	酷喔！是CD耶！派對上請自便喔！
B: Yeah! Don't worry! **I** will **enjoy myself**!	好啊！別擔心！我會在派對上玩得很開心的！

超萬用單字／句型

▸ Help yourself.

這句是美國人常用的招待用語，可以解釋為「自己來吧。」具有告訴對方不用客氣的意義，如同中文裡告訴對方不需要拘束有相同的意思。最常使用於用餐時。

❶ **A: Just help yourself. There are still a lot of dishes coming up.** → 別客氣儘管自己來吧。我們等一下還有很多好吃的呢。

B: Thank you very much. → 非常謝謝你的好意。

❷ **A: Here is your room; just help yourself settle in.**
→ 這是你的房間，自己安頓一下吧。

B: Alright, thanks. → 好的，謝謝。

▸ I enjoyed myself.

不同於上面的那句，這一句是用來回應對方招待的用語。可以解釋為「我玩得很開心。」用來回應對方熱情的招待。通常在派對或活動之後便可以對主辦人說這句話來感謝對方的用心。

❶ **A: Hey Emma! How did you like today's gathering?**
→ 嗨，艾瑪！你喜歡今天的聚會嗎？

B: Yes, I enjoyed myself very much. Thank you.
→ 嗯，我玩得很開心。謝謝。

❷ **A: I really enjoyed myself at the party. Thank you, Allen.**
→ 今天的派對我真的玩得很開心，謝謝你的招待，艾倫。

B: I am glad to hear that. Thank you for coming, too.
→ 我很高興聽到你這麼說。也謝謝你來參加。

實用句型大補帖

1 **Hey guys! Come on in and have a seat. The party will start in a few minutes.**
嘿，大夥！趕快進來找地方坐吧。派對再幾分鐘就開始了。

2 **Kate's birthday party was awesome!**
凱特的生日派對超讚的！

3 **Are you going to Tom's party this Sunday?**
你這星期天會去參加湯姆的生日派對嗎？

4 **Everyone, let's eat! There is pizza, salad, cookies and drinks. Just help yourself.**
大家趕快來吃吧！這裡有披薩、沙拉、餅乾和飲料，自己拿吧。

5 **Come on, let's sing the birthday song for John! Hurry! Light up the candles on the cake first, and turn off the lights. Let's gather around the table.**
大家來替約翰唱生日快樂歌！快點先把蛋糕上的蠟燭點起來，把燈關掉，然後大家圍在桌子邊吧。

6 **Make your wishes ! Don't forget to tell us the first two wishes,and you have to keep the last one a secret.**
許願吧！別忘了告訴我們前兩個願望，然後把最後一個留著保密。

7 **I am thinking about what I should get for Jenny for her birthday present.**
我在想要買什麼給珍妮當作她的生日禮物。

8 **Are you free this Saturday, Amy? If you don't mind I just want to ask if you would like to come to my birthday party.**
艾咪，你這個星期六有空嗎？如果你不介意的話，我想邀請你來參加我的生日派對。

9 **I really enjoyed myself! Thank you so much for inviting me.**
我真的玩得很開心！謝謝你今天邀請我。

Unit 5

Halloween

——萬聖節——

和每個人都聊得來 Track 058

加粗底線字：詳見「超萬用單字／句型」

A: Tomorrow is Halloween. Do you want to help me make a jack-o'-lantern?	明天就是萬聖節了。你願意幫我做個南瓜燈嗎？
B: I'd love to. I heard about Halloween when I was in Beijing. It's kind of like Children's Day.	我願意，我在北京時就聽說萬聖節了，聽起來就像是兒童節。
A: Yep! Small kids get dressed up, then walk around with paper bags or baskets knocking on their neighbor's doors. They always say: "Trick or Treat?"	小孩們喬裝打扮好後就帶著紙袋或者籃子四處敲鄰居們的門。他們會說：「不給糖就搗蛋！」
B: That's kind of cool! But will the kids really play a trick if they don't get candies?	真有意思，但是如果沒拿到糖果，孩子們真的會搗蛋嗎？
A: Yeah, usually it's the older kids going around playing pranks.	通常是一些比較大的孩子們到處走動來做一些惡作劇。
B: It sounds like a lot of fun! Maybe I could get together with my friends and try it out that night!	聽起來太有意思了，也許那晚我也可以和我的朋友們一起玩這個！
A: Uh…but, the adults usually don't go around trick-or-treating like kids. Instead they hold a big party and get dressed up, too.	呃……但是成年人通常不玩孩子們的遊街活動，他們會舉辦一個大的派對，當然也要喬裝打扮了。

B:	Fantastic! **I would say** that we should hold our own party!	太讚了！我覺得我們應該來辦個自己的派對！
A:	I'd like to, but I haven't prepared anything to dress up with. **How about you?**	我很想，但我還沒準備裝扮用的任何用品，你呢？
B:	Well, not yet, either. Let's get something for dressing up now!	嗯，也還沒有準備好。我們現在一起去準備吧！

超萬用單字／句型

▶ I would say...

此句片語可解釋為「我會說……」是一句用來根據事情來表達自己的意見。通常用於當別人詢問自己意見或要發表看法，便可以用 I would say 當作開頭。同時也具有「我認為」「我覺得」之意。

❶ **A: What do you think about what Jack and Louis said?**
→ 你對於傑克和路易斯說的話有什麼看法？
B: I would say that Jack probably didn't tell the truth.
→ 我會說，傑克恐怕沒有說出事實。

❷ **A: What should we do at this point?** → 我們現在該怎麼做呢？
B: I would say we should calm down and think again carefully. → 我想，我們應該冷靜下來好好再思考一遍。

▶ How about you?

可以簡單的解釋為「那你覺得呢？」是一句用在詢問對方意見及意願時所使用的問句。較其他詢問方式相比聽起來較為和善而輕鬆。

❶ **A: We are going to buy something to eat. How about you?**
→ 我們要去買些吃的。你呢？
B: I think I will cook by myself. → 我想我會自己煮。

❷ **A: I like the red one better. How about you?**
→ 我比較喜歡紅色的，你覺得呢？
B: I think it is ok. → 我覺得還可以。

實用句型大補帖

1 **I love Halloween very much. I think it is the coolest festival!**
我超愛萬聖節的。我覺得那是最酷的節日了！

2 **I would say that every child should be excited about Halloween, because you can dress up to be anything you like, and you can get candies by scaring people.**
我說每個小孩一定都會為萬聖節感到興奮，因為你可以打扮成任何你所喜歡的樣子，然後嚇人還可以拿到糖果。

3 **John is going to dress up as a pirate, it should be cool I guess. How about you, Lisa?**
約翰準備扮成海盜，我想那應該很酷。那你呢，麗莎？

4 **We are going to buy our costumes for the Halloween party tomorrow night. Do you want to come with us? Then we will do our make-up at Cindy's house together tomorrow afternoon.**
我們要去買明天晚上萬聖節派對要穿的服裝。你想跟我們一起去嗎？然後我們明天下午一起去辛蒂家化妝。

5 **Did you hear about the haunted house that we are going to go to tomorrow for Halloween?**
你聽說明天我們要去的萬聖節的鬼屋了嗎？

6 **"Trick or Treat?" is a popular phrase on Halloween. You can see children holding a small pumpkin bucket and saying this to anyone they see to get candies.**
「不給糖就搗蛋！」是萬聖節必定會聽到的口號。你可以看到小孩子們都拿著南瓜形狀的小桶子，向碰到的每個人說這句話要糖果。

7 **Cutting a pumpkin face is a traditional activity on Halloween, too. My grandma always does that each year. She said without cutting pumpkins, Halloween is not a perfect Halloween.**
製作南瓜鬼臉也是萬聖節的傳統活動之一。我的祖母每年都會做。她說不切南瓜的話，萬聖節就不算是完美的萬聖節了。

8 **No matter those scary decorations or the haunted houses, everything about the festival makes me excited.**
不管是那些恐怖的裝飾還是鬼屋，所有關於萬聖節的一切都讓我很興奮。

9 **Pumpkin pies are the traditional food for Halloween; almost every family has that on their menu for their Halloween feast.**
南瓜派是萬聖節的傳統食物，幾乎每個家庭的萬聖節大餐裡都會有這道菜。

Unit 6

Thanksgiving

——感恩節——

和每個人都聊得來 Track 059

加粗底線字：詳見「超萬用單字／句型」

A: Happy Thanksgiving Day!	感恩節快樂！
B: Happy Thanksgiving Day! Do you have any plans for today?	感恩節快樂！今天你有什麼計畫嗎？
A: Not really, all my friends are going home, like during Chinese New Year. What are you going to do?	沒有，我所有的朋友都回家，就像中國的春節一樣，你打算做什麼呢？
B: I'll go to my friend Eva's home and spend the day with her and her family!	我會去我朋友伊娃的家，然後在那裡和她還有她的家人過感恩節！
A: You mean your American friend Eva? You'll **enjoy your break** at her house?	妳說妳的美國朋友，伊娃嗎？你會去她家度過美好的節日假期嗎？
B: Yep! If you're interested, you can come with me and my friend to Eva's home. Her whole family will be there.	如果你感興趣的話，你可以和我還有我的朋友一起去伊娃的家過感恩節，伊娃全家都會在。
A: That's very kind. Thanks. I'd love to come.	真的太好了，我很願意
B: I'm glad you're coming. **You can't miss** the chance to see how American families spend their Thanksgiving.	我很高興你會來，你不能錯過這個好機會，去看看美國家庭怎麼過感恩節。
A: Could you tell me something about it?	你能談談感恩節嗎？

B: It's usually a big family reunion day. They always have lots of delicious food, like turkey and stuffing. They have yams, corn, carrots and fruit pies or pumpkin pies.	感恩節通常都是家庭的團聚的大日子。他們會做很多好吃的比如火雞。他們還吃馬鈴薯、玉米、胡蘿蔔和水果派或南瓜派。

超萬用單字／句型

▶You can't miss...

這句的意思可解釋為「你絕對不能錯過……」具有強調的語氣，常用於強調東西獨特、品質好，一定要試試看就可以用這句。

❶ **A: You can't miss the Broadway shows if you are going to New York.** → 如果你要去紐約，就一定不能錯過百老匯的表演。

B: I will definitely go see one. → 我一定會去看看的。

❷ **A: The parade is one thing you can't miss when going to Disneyland!** → 去迪士尼樂園的話就一定不能錯過花車嘉年華遊行！

B: Yes, I heard it is awesome. → 好，我聽說那個很棒。

▶Enjoy your break!

這是一句外國人常用的片語，用來祝福對方假期玩得愉快。美國常會使用類似的片語如 Have a nice day!（祝你有美好的一天！）或是 Enjoy yourself!（祝你玩得盡興！）來祝福對方。

❶ **A: I heard you are going to San Diego for the winter vacation. Enjoy your break!** → 我聽說你寒假要去聖地牙哥，祝你假期愉快！

B: Thank you. → 謝謝你的祝福。

❷ **A: Enjoy your break and see you after summer!**
→ 祝你假期愉快然後暑假之後見！

B: Thank you, you too.
→ 謝謝，你也是。

實用句型大補帖

1 **Thanksgiving is time for families to get together and have a nice meal!**
感恩節是個讓家人可以一起團聚，好好吃頓大餐的日子。

2 **All the family members will come back, including Uncle Sam! I haven't seen him and his family for ages.**
全部的親戚都會回來，包括山姆叔叔，我已經好久沒看到他和他的家人了。

3 **My brother and my mother went to the supermarket to shop for Thanksgiving. I hope they can bring some beer back, too.**
我弟弟和我媽媽去超市買感恩節要用的東西了。我希望他們能順便帶些啤酒回來。

4 **Turkey is one of the traditional foods every family must have on their table for Thanksgiving! By the way, the fruit pie is delicious, too! You can't miss these two in order to have a great Thanksgiving meal!**
火雞是每個家庭必備的感恩節佳餚！另外，水果派也非常美味！想要有一頓美好的感恩節大餐就絕對不能錯過這兩道料理！

5 **We are going to church tomorrow. It is important to worship God on such a religious holiday.**
我們明天要去教堂，在這個充滿宗教氣氛的節日做禮拜是很重要的一件事。

6 **Usually many young people who are currently living out will go back home to spend time with their families.**
通常在外的年輕人都會回家和家人過節。

7 **I will go back to Los Angeles because my grandfather is there, and we have a family trip.**
我會回去洛杉磯，因為我祖父在那裡，然後我們有一趟家族旅遊。

8 **Many people couldn't get on their flights and were trapped in the airport for the holiday.**
很多人沒辦法搭上班機而被迫困在機場度過假日了。

9 **I am going to order a flight ticket to Texas, since my mother really wants me to go back home to spend the break with them.**
我準備訂機票回德州，因為我媽很想要我回去和他們一起過節。

10 **Happy thanksgiving! Enjoy your break!**
感恩節快樂，祝你假期愉快！

Unit 7

Christmas

——聖誕節——

和每個人都聊得來 Track 060

加粗底線字：詳見「超萬用單字／句型」

A: It seems that the whole city has gone Christmas mad!	似乎整個城市都在為聖誕節瘋狂！
B: Why do you say that?	為什麼這麼說呢？
A: Everywhere I go, I see Christmas decorations, and hear Christmas songs!	我走到哪裡看到的都是聖誕飾品、聽到的都是聖誕歌。
B: Well, **this is how** Christmas **should be like.** Don't you think that decorations and songs are two important things of Christmas?	嗯，聖誕節就是要這樣啊。你不覺得聖誕飾品跟聖誕歌是聖誕節兩個重要的元素嗎？
A: God! All I **ask for** is just a piece of silence. Why is it so hard these days?	天啊！我只不過想要一點寧靜而已，怎麼最近這麼難啊？
B: Let's stop complaining! Have you sent out Christmas cards?	我們別抱怨了吧！你的聖誕卡寄了嗎？
A: You know that I tend to be well organized. I posted them two weeks ago.	你知道我做事一向條理分明。兩個星期前我已經寄出卡片了！
B: What about Christmas shopping? Don't tell me you have already done that as well!	那聖誕禮物的採買呢？別告訴我你也已經採買完畢了！

A: I did all of that in July during the sales, and saved a lot.	我在七月大特價的時候，就全都買完了，我還省了不少錢呢。
B: Gosh! I have so much more to learn from you!	老天爺啊！我要跟你學的太多了！

超萬用單字／句型

▶ask for...

這句可以解釋為「向他人詢問……」，具有向他人求助的意義。最常聽到的 ask for help 便是向他人尋求幫忙之意。另外此片語後方可帶入其他名詞便可明確指出欲詢問對方的試務及需要的幫忙。

❶ **A: God, I think we are lost. I don't know where this place is.**
→ 天哪，我想我們迷路了。我不知道這是哪裡。
B: Don't panic, let's just ask someone for directions, ok?
→ 別驚慌，讓我們來問一下路就行了，好嗎？

❷ **A: This closet is too heavy. We need to ask for more people to help us move it.**
→ 這個衣櫃太重了。我們需要找更多的人來幫我們搬。
B: I think so, too. Let me get someone.
→ 我想也是，我去找些人來。

▶This is how...should be like.

這句的語法偏向語助詞的修辭類，帶有讚美雀躍之意。可解釋為「就應該是這樣！」句型中直接帶入欲修飾的名詞即可。

❶ **A: God! I am so busy and tired every day.**
→ 天啊！我每天都又忙又累。
B: Well, this is how work should be like. → 嗯，這就是工作啊。

❷ **A: Look at those kindergarten kids. How cute they are!**
→ 看看那些幼稚園的孩子，多可愛啊！
B: Yes, this is how children should be like.
→ 是啊，小孩子就是應該這樣。

實用句型大補帖

1. **Merry Christmas!**
聖誕快樂！

2. **We are decorating the Christmas tree; we put a lot of cute little things on the tree, such as snowmen, bells, and Santa Claus.**
我們正在布置聖誕樹。我們放了很多可愛的小東西在樹上，像是雪人、鈴鐺和聖誕老人等等。

3. **My mom wants to hang a Christmas wreath on the door.**
我媽媽想在門上掛聖誕花圈。

4. **Children love Christmas so bad, because they believe that Santa Claus really exists and will bring them gifts on Christmas Eve.**
小孩子們都愛死聖誕節了，因為他們相信真的有聖誕老人，而且聖誕老人會在平安夜的時候送禮物給他們。

5. **I want to buy a chocolate cake for Christmas; do you want to go with me?**
我想買一個聖誕節巧克力蛋糕，你想和我一起去嗎？

6. **There are always Santa Clauses at the shopping malls for people to take pictures with during Christmas. It is fun to watch. Some children loved it but some eventually cried.**
每次只要聖誕節來臨，百貨公司裡總會有聖誕老人可以一起拍照。那看起來很有趣。有些小朋友表現得很開心，但是有些卻會哭出來。

7. **There are usually people from charities asking for donations during Christmas. Sometimes, I will give them a dollar or so.**
聖誕節的時候，總會有許多慈善機構募捐。有的時候我會給他們一兩塊。

8. **I will go back home to see my grandparents first, and then I will head South with my family, because it is warmer there. We want to enjoy a sunny Christmas.**
我會先回家看我的祖父母，然後再和我的家人前往南部，因為那邊比較暖和。我們想要享受陽光聖誕節。

9. **I love the snow, because this is how Christmas should be like! We should make a snowman outside!**
我很愛下雪，聖誕節就是應該這樣！我們應該在外面堆個雪人！

10. **I have already received some cards from several of my friends.**
我已經收到從一些朋友那裡寄來的卡片了。

NOTE

NOTE

原來如此 系列 E241

初學必備！一個月就能和任何人輕鬆聊的英文會話

於無形中輕鬆學會日常生活中最常用的英語會話

作　　者　張螢安 ◎著
顧　　問　曾文旭
社　　長　王毓芳
編輯統籌　耿文國
主　　編　吳靜宜
執行編輯　吳佳芬、廖婉婷、黃韻璇
美術編輯　王桂芳、張嘉容
封面設計　阿作
法律顧問　北辰著作權事務所　蕭雄淋律師、幸秋妙律師

初　　版　2021年01月
出　　版　捷徑文化出版事業有限公司
電　　話　(02)2752-5618
傳　　真　(02)2752-5619

定　　價　新台幣340元／港幣113元
產品內容　1書

總 經 銷　采舍國際有限公司
地　　址　235 新北市中和區中山路二段366巷10號3樓
電　　話　（02）8245-8786
傳　　真　（02）8245-8718

港澳地區總經銷　和平圖書有限公司
地　　址　香港柴灣嘉業街12號百樂門大廈17樓
電　　話　(852)2804-6687
傳　　真　(852)2804-6409

▶本書部分圖片由 Shutterstock、freepik 圖庫提供。

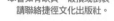

國家圖書館出版品預行編目資料

初學必備！一個月就能和任何人輕鬆聊的英文會話 / 張螢安著. -- 初版. -- 臺北市：捷徑文化, 2021.01
面；　公分（原來如此：E241）
ISBN 978-986-5507-50-3(平裝)
1. 英語　2. 會話
805.188　　109018874